"Oh, no, you d [ear. "You're no] **that easily."**

"Tanner." His name came out in a relieved cough. "There's a fire. I heard a noise and I think someone was calling my name. It's behind that door."

"That was *me* calling your name. We've got to go."

She gestured toward the door. "But what about the noise? There may be someone trapped in there."

The screeching noise got higher and louder and Tanner muttered a curse under his breath, tucking his arm around her and launching her toward the corner. They just made it around and she was about to argue her case again when a thundering explosion roared from where they'd just been standing. Smoke encased the hall from top to bottom.

"Wh-what—" Bree stuttered.

"Too many accelerants in a construction area. It was like a pressure cooker."

A pressure cooker that would've killed her if Tanner hadn't been there to stop her from opening that door.

RISK
EVERYTHING

USA TODAY Bestselling Author
JANIE CROUCH

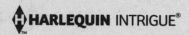
HARLEQUIN INTRIGUE®

This book is dedicated to Marci Mathers. Thank you for the years of support and friendship. You mean the world to me.

ISBN-13: 978-1-335-60465-1

Risk Everything

Recycling programs for this product may not exist in your area.

Printed in U.S.A.

www.Harlequin.com

Janie Crouch has loved to read romance her whole life. This *USA TODAY* bestselling author cut her teeth on Harlequin Romance novels as a preteen, then moved on to a passion for romantic suspense as an adult. Janie lives with her husband and four children overseas. She enjoys traveling, long-distance running, movie watching, knitting and adventure/obstacle racing. You can find out more about her at janiecrouch.com.

Books by Janie Crouch

Harlequin Intrigue

The Risk Series:
A Bree and Tanner Thriller

Calculated Risk
Security Risk
Constant Risk
Risk Everything

Omega Sector:
Under Siege

Daddy Defender
Protector's Instinct
Cease Fire

Omega Sector:
Critical Response

Special Forces Savior
Fully Committed
Armored Attraction
Man of Action
Overwhelming Force
Battle Tested

Omega Sector

Infiltration
Countermeasures
Untraceable
Leverage

Primal Instinct

Visit the Author Profile page at Harlequin.com.

CAST OF CHARACTERS

Tanner Dempsey—Deputy captain of the Grand County, Colorado, sheriff's office; lives and works in Risk Peak.

Bree Daniels—Shy computer genius, now living and working in Risk Peak teaching computer classes at the New Journeys women's shelter.

Noah Dempsey—Tanner's brother; former Special Forces, owns a ranch with Tanner.

Marilyn Ellis—Single mother who works at New Journeys.

Sam and Eva Ellis—Marilyn's young son and daughter.

Jared Ellis—Marilyn's abusive husband; currently awaiting trial.

Cassandra Dempsey Martin—Tanner and Noah's sister; runs New Journeys with Bree.

Chapter One

In the past year Bree Daniels had been chased across the country, shot at, kidnapped, almost blown up, strangled and had watched the man she loved almost bleed to death right in front of her.

But she could honestly say none of that was as treacherous as what she was going through now.

Planning her wedding.

Seriously. When a bad guy with a gun or a knife came at you, you knew you were in trouble. But nobody suspected that agreeing to get married and giving the ladies of the small town where you'd made your home free rein in planning said nuptials was also just as dangerous.

If they were ever arrested, wedding planners would need their own special section in prison. In isolation. Because otherwise they would take over and rule the place, for sure.

For the past seven months the women of Risk Peak—mostly Cassandra, her good friend and future sister-in-law, and Cheryl, owner of the Sunrise Diner and surrogate mother to Bree—had tracked Bree down, no matter where she'd tried to hide, demanding answers to impossible questions of all types.

Like what kinds of flower arrangements Bree wanted. And whether she wanted a custard cream, buttercream or whipped cream to go along with the raspberry ganache in the cake.

When Bree had finally had a chance to look up what a ganache was, she wanted to throw her computer across the room. Why the heck hadn't they just said raspberry *filling*?

The ladies were so enthusiastic about the event that Bree wasn't even sure they would notice if she fled the state.

The thought had crossed her mind.

But she was trying to be more *normal*. Normal women were excited about all this wedding planning, right? Cassandra had shown her the scrapbook she'd made from the ages of seven to eighteen. That thing had roughly four million pages of pictures of wedding gowns, color schemes, flower types and bridesmaids' dresses.

Bree had mentioned there were much better ways to organize the information electronically, but Cassandra had just rolled her eyes and said that wasn't the point.

Bree wasn't exactly sure what was the point, but she knew that most women were a lot more excited about this whole planning process than she was.

Bree just wanted to be Mrs. Tanner Dempsey. She wished she could go back in time and punch her past self in the face for not taking him up on his offer/threat to drag her in front of the nearest county judge and get married right away after they'd gotten engaged.

Well, the *second* time they'd gotten engaged.

The first time he'd asked her it had been right after a monster from her past had almost blown them both up. They'd been covered in smoke, bleeding and a little shaky on their feet. But Tanner had dropped to one knee right there and asked her to marry him, not wanting to wait a second longer.

The second time, a few weeks later on Valentine's Day, Tanner had taken her deep into the land of the ranch they both loved and asked her again—so romantically—at sunset, the gorgeous Rocky Mountains in the distance.

He'd explained that when she told their grandkids about how he'd asked her to marry him, he wanted this to be the story she would tell.

She planned to tell *both*.

But the next day when Tanner had threatened to drag her to get married *right then*, she should've taken him up on it.

Maybe then she wouldn't be going through the most vicious of wedding planning torture: the gown fittings. The gown *everything*. She'd almost rather be on the run for her life than be twisted, pulled on, poked and prodded and, worst of all, *oohed* over.

"My brother is going to lose his…*stuff* when he sees you in this wedding gown."

Cassandra Dempsey Martin was the only person

Bree knew who could out curse a seasoned sailor yet still be in tears at the sight of the wedding gown.

Cheryl grabbed Cassandra's hand that was fluttering emotionally in midair and nodded. "Oh, honey, it really does look more gorgeous every time you put it on."

Bree grimaced. "It's just so much money to spend on a dress that I'm only going to wear once. That's just so impractical. Why would I do this?"

It went against every instinct Bree had to be impractical. She was nothing if not logical, orderly and pragmatic.

Cassandra rolled her eyes. "It's your *wedding dress*. It's supposed to be impractical. Because if you do it right, you only do it once. Because you deserve to wear a beautiful gown walking down the aisle. And besides, it's really not that much for a wedding dress. Most gowns cost five times that much."

Bree just stared at herself in the three-way mirror. She had to admit, it was a beautiful, elaborate dress. It made her waist seem trimmer, and her hips, which had filled out to a much more feminine shape over the last few months since she was eating regularly and not on the run for her life, flared nicely under the material.

But it was too fancy. Too much lace. Too many sequins. Too much of that itchy white stuff. It was a gorgeous gown, but it just wasn't *her*. She shouldn't have let herself be talked into it, but Cheryl and Dan—the people who had taken her in when she first arrived in Risk Peak basically living out of her car—had insisted on buying her a gown. Then Bree had made the mistake of taking Cassandra and a group of their friends shopping with her for one.

She'd put this gown on in the dressing room with the associate's help and then almost taken it back off again. It was too fancy. But the damned associate had talked her into showing it to her friends.

There was so much crying and cursing from her friends when they saw the dress, Bree figured they must know something she didn't. And when it came to dresses, that was a lot. So she'd gotten it.

And it was still just as beautiful. She couldn't deny that.

Plus, if she was honest, she could admit it wasn't really even the dress that had her in such a tizzy. It was the fact that in two weeks she was going to have to stand up in front of over five hundred people—that was more people than she'd ever talked to in her entire life *combined*—and say her vows to Tanner. Vows they'd agreed to personalize and write themselves.

If Bree speaking in front of a huge group of people about her emotions wasn't a recipe for disaster, she didn't know what was. The elegant bride in the beautiful dress looking back at her from the mirror broke out into a sweat at the thought.

She'd been engaged to Tanner for seven months. In love with him since almost the first moment she'd met him months before that. But she was only just now getting to the point where she could make coherent sentences about her emotions directly to him *alone*. He didn't seem to mind when she stuttered over words or blurted out often socially inappropriate declarations. He took it in stride and had learned how to "speak Bree fluently," as he called it.

But it wouldn't be just Tanner at the wedding in two weeks. It would be a bunch of people who *didn't* speak Bree fluently. She was going to make a complete fool out of herself and embarrass him. She already knew it. And didn't see any way to get around it.

"Hey, do you really not like it that much? You look gorgeous." Cassandra made eye contact with Bree in the mirror as she peeked over her shoulder.

"No, it's not the dress." Not *just* the dress, although the dress was pretty much an icon for the fraud Bree felt like. "It's the whole wedding. I'm just not good at this stuff, you know that."

Cassandra grinned. "You're not giving yourself enough credit for how far you've come in the last few months. Think about what we've done with New Journeys."

Cheryl smiled her encouragement too. "A far cry from that exhausted woman who fell asleep at the diner table over a year ago."

The seamstress came in and positioned Bree's arms to do the pinnings for the final fitting. Cassandra was right in a lot of ways. When Bree moved here a year ago, she'd barely known how to talk to anyone. Now she was helping run a very successful women's shelter program. It had grown so big that a few months ago they'd had to move into a larger facility.

"New Journeys still doesn't mean I'm not going to make a complete idiot out of myself in front of the town during the ceremony." Bree spun in the opposite direction when the seamstress motioned for her to do so. "Good thing we're not going to split the aisles between the bride's side and the groom's side. My side would be so empty we might tip over the whole church."

Bree's only family was her cousin Melissa. She and her husband, Chris, and their twin nineteen-month-olds were coming, and Bree was so thrilled to see the babies that had first brought her and Tanner together. But it still didn't make up for the fact that Tanner had been born and raised in Risk Peak and knew half the residents of Grand County personally.

Cassandra shook her head. "You know people here love you. Mom would probably sit on your side. I definitely would. We both like you better than Tanner anyway."

Bree laughed as the seamstress finished her pinning and began to carefully take off the lovely gown. Cassandra was right—the people in Risk Peak cared about her. She needed to remember that.

And try to live through her own wedding.

An hour later, Bree and Cassandra were pulling up to the three-story office building on the outskirts of Risk Peak that had been converted into apartments and bedrooms for the shelter. The stress from the wedding planning and dress fitting melted away when Bree saw it. This place gave her purpose. This place made a difference in women's lives.

Bree knew what it was like to live in fear and feel like she had no options. If she could help take that same heavy sense of despair from another woman, she would gladly do it. She'd been teaching computer skills to the women at New Journeys for the past seven months; Cassandra offered training in basic cosmetology for those interested in that route.

Cassandra and Bree walked in the main front door that opened into the hallway and expansive living room of New Journeys. The living room was giant— they'd deliberately knocked out a number of walls when they remodeled the place to give the room a wide-open feel. A television sat in one corner with a couch and a couple of chairs around it. A second corner had been turned into a giant reading nook, with books of every kind and for every age. The other end of the room held a table with a half-completed jigsaw puzzle and board games stacked on a corner shelf.

This was the family room, even for the people here, many of whom struggled to understand what a family was supposed to feel like. Family was another concept Bree hadn't understood very well before meeting Tanner and coming to live in Risk Peak.

She hung her lightweight jacket on a wall hook and looked around. Even May in Colorado could be cool. Everything was as it should be—loud and relaxed. Women talking, kids laughing, the TV on in the background, the dog running around in circles after its own tail. Late afternoon tended to be a boisterous time around here.

"Bree Cheese!"

Bree smiled at the sound of the two small voices calling her name from the table and chairs over in the corner. It was one of her favorite sounds in the entire world.

Sam and Eva, seven and five years old respectively, were the two children of Marilyn Ellis. They'd lived here for four months with their mom.

Marilyn had been Bree's best computer student to date. Even though the woman hadn't graduated from high school, nor gone to college, she picked up the computer classes Bree taught with the ease of a natural.

And had also become one of Bree's good friends to the point that she was even going to be a bridesmaid in her wedding. Little Eva was going to be the flower girl.

"You guys should let Miss Bree get in the door before you start screaming your heads off for her," Marilyn admonished softly. Marilyn did everything softly. In the four months Bree had known her, she had never once heard the other woman raise her voice.

Bree didn't know everything about Marilyn's situation before she arrived in Risk Peak, but she knew her husband had put her in the hospital and was now awaiting trial. Marilyn and the kids had been some of the first residents at New Journeys. And when they'd opened the new facility, Marilyn had agreed to take a full-time job as the building facilitator and sort of den mom.

She excelled at it.

"Of course I want to see these two as soon as I come in the door." Bree pulled the kids in for a hug. "Who wouldn't want a squad of rug rats chanting their name first thing?"

And it was true. To see how Eva and Sam were blossoming made it worth any possible crazy name the kids might call her. Including Bree Cheese, which had been the compromise between them calling her Bree the way she had wanted, and Miss Daniels, the way Marilyn wanted.

"Schoolwork, you two. Got to make sure you're ready for next week's camping trip." Marilyn pointed back to the table. The kids moaned and tromped forward like they were headed to the guillotine.

Bree laughed at their dramatics, delighting in it. Just a few months ago they would've never acted that way. "Their teacher must be pretty mean."

Marilyn gave a small smile. She was their teacher since she'd decided to teach them at home for the rest of this school year rather than add the trauma of a new school to an already traumatic year. "They're so excited about the camping, I can hardly get an hour's worth of work out of them."

"Understandable." Bree smiled once more.

"Everything okay here while we were gone?" Cassandra asked.

"Nothing of particular interest. That pipe in the hall bath is still leaking a little."

"And no word about Jared?" Bree asked softly.

Marilyn flinched at the sound of her estranged husband's name before smoothing her features. "Nothing either way."

Jared's lawyer was trying to get him out on bail, something Marilyn definitely didn't want happening.

"Okay, good." Bree nodded. "Keep us posted."

"I will. Although finding out details isn't easy. Ironically, because of privacy issues." Marilyn sighed softly and looked over at Eva and Sam. "The kids are sad that Chandler is gone."

Bree met Cassandra's eyes and then looked at Marilyn, all of them giving resigned nods. Chandler's mother, Angel, had been here three weeks. Two days ago, she'd decided to move back in with her boyfriend, despite the violent situation that had originally caused her to leave in the first place.

Angel said her boyfriend had changed. Had made promises.

Bree didn't know which was harder: seeing the hope in the other woman's eyes or knowing that the chances her boyfriend had changed after multiple years of abuse were pretty nonexistent.

And poor Chandler was caught in the middle of it all.

It wasn't the first time someone from New Journeys had decided to return to a less than optimal situation. It had taken both Bree and Cassandra quite a bit of time to come to grips with the fact that not everyone could make the permanent break from their abusive situations. For some, the unknown was harder to deal with than the pain.

But it still sometimes broke Bree's heart.

All they could do was provide what they could: a safe place and a new set of skills so that these women could support themselves, get back up on their feet and move on with their lives.

People like Marilyn were a prime example of why places like New Journeys was needed. She had made a huge difference in her own life once she had just a little help. But it was also needed for people like Angel who found the steps so much more difficult to take.

Bree and Cassandra grabbed cups of coffee, and they all came back into the family room to chat about all the daily things that needed tending to here. Half the building still hadn't been renovated yet. New Journeys had quite a bit of private funding thanks to the Matarazzo family, who worked with some law enforcement group named Omega Sector in Colorado Springs, but renovating everything at once would have been too much to handle on multiple levels.

They currently had sixteen residents in the building, about three-quarters of its current capacity, and roughly one-third of what the building would be able to house once all the renovations were finished.

New Journeys had gone out of their way to make themselves particularly welcoming to women with children, so over half of the residents now had children with them—babies up through middle-school age.

Which explained the noise level in the room right

now. None of the three women paid much attention to it. Cassandra and Marilyn were used to it since they had their own kids, and Bree just loved the chaos of it all.

But when the room fell almost completely silent a few moments later she sadly knew what had happened. A man had walked into the room. Bree forced herself not to tense or turn around to see who it was. How she reacted would influence how everyone else reacted.

Cassandra winked at her—able to see who was in the doorway—and a half smile pulled at Bree's face as she heard giggles a few moments later. She knew exactly what man had walked into the room.

Hers.

Chapter Two

Tanner kept his stance neutral, his posture relaxed as he made his way into the silent room. Susan, one of the residents here, knew him and had let him in the side kitchen door when he'd knocked.

Nobody got into New Journeys who wasn't invited. Every door had double reinforced locks and a security code. Nobody could just wander in from the streets and enter the building. With all the time Bree spent here, and with as many violent offenders the residents of New Journeys had contact with, Tanner had personally made sure of it.

Tanner knew the code, of course, and had a key to let himself in if there was an emergency, but he'd never done so. The women and children who lived here needed to know they were safe from both danger and from uninvited men just wandering around, even those who didn't mean harm.

Case in point, the silence that fell over the large living room when he entered. Every child stopped what they were doing—playing, homework, talking—and stared at him.

He wasn't sure if his Grand County Sheriff's Office uniform helped or hindered his attempt to set a positive example of what a man should be. Some of these women and children had received no help from law enforcement when they'd needed it most.

He stood in the doorway for a long moment, a smile on his face, arms resting loosely at his sides as everyone processed who he was and that he meant no one here any harm. It didn't take them more than a couple of seconds to get past their instinctive fear.

He grinned as big as he could, then brought his finger up to his lips, telling all the kids to keep quiet. Using exaggerated motions, he pretended to sneak up behind Bree. The kids began to giggle, knowing both Cassandra and Marilyn could see him and weren't concerned, so they didn't have to be either.

"You can't escape the kissing monster," he said in a deep, Muppet-sounding voice. He began pecking at the top of her head, her cheeks, her shoulders, from where she sat in the chair at the table.

Bree played along, like he'd known she would. "Oh, no, not the kissing monster."

Giggles broke out all over the room, then turned into laughing noises of disgust as Bree finally turned her head up and Tanner kissed her—very chastely—on the lips.

It was their routine. It had started out in jest, but when they'd realized how much some of these children, and their moms, needed to see men in a more easygoing, positive light, it had become a regular part of their day as Tanner picked her up to escort her home.

The noise in the room fell back to its dull roar, everyone returning to their activities now that the show was over, as Bree stood up and smiled at him.

Those green eyes still gutted him just as much now as they had the first time he saw her shoplifting in the drugstore over a year ago.

"Hi," she whispered.

He looped an arm around her waist and pulled her close, but he didn't kiss her the way he wanted to, mindful of the audience who might not be actively watching but were still aware of their every move. "Hi, yourself. Good day?"

He knew she'd had a wedding dress fitting today, and that that event tended to stress her out.

But he was also a man and knew better than to try to offer any advice or help. That would probably just get him killed. Not by Bree, but definitely by Cassandra or one of the other women in the throes of wedding planning bliss.

"Let's just say I'll be happy two weeks from now when all this is over and I never have to be the center of attention again."

He trailed a finger down her cheek and leaned closer to make sure no one could hear them. "You may not be the center of the town's attention, but I can promise you that once you are Mrs. Dempsey, you very definitely will be the center of my attention."

He loved how her breath hitched and her mouth formed a little O shape.

"Hey, you two," Cassandra's voice rang out. "There are little eyes everywhere."

Tanner was well aware of that. It was the only reason he didn't have Bree pushed up against the wall kissing the life out of her.

He forced himself to take a step back. "I'll behave."

The look of disappointment on Bree's face was almost the death of him. Whoever's idea it had been not to have sex for the last two months before their wedding was a complete idiot.

Oh, yeah, that was him.

He forced himself to step away and sat down to talk about New Journeys and any issues. What happened here affected him on multiple levels. Personally, because of his tie to Bree and Cassandra. Professionally, because he was the captain of the sheriff's department for this section of the county. Whatever he could do to help keep these women safe and secure, he was more than willing to do.

Sometimes that meant grabbing a hammer and drill and helping hang some pictures or adjust some light fixtures. Tanner didn't mind. As a matter of fact, he and his brother, Noah, had been spending quite a few hours here during their time off. Both of them also realized that they were doing a lot more than some random honey-do list items by showing up week after week. They were trying, in some small way, to reclaim part of what had been lost by the years of violence perpetrated against the residents here.

It wasn't enough. Wouldn't ever be enough. But at least it was something.

Bree was talking schedules with Cassandra and Marilyn when Tanner felt a tug on his sleeve. He knew who it was before he even looked by how Marilyn's eyes tracked the entire situation.

"Why, hello there, princess."

Eva smiled up at him. "Hi, Captain Lips."

Tanner managed not to grimace at his nickname. Bree had made the mistake of calling him by her private nickname for him—Captain Hot Lips—in front of Cassandra. His sister, never one to let a humiliating situation die naturally, started calling him that all the time. But at least the kids had overheard only part of it, and thus the nickname Captain Lips.

But this sweet child could call him anything she wanted if it meant she felt free enough to come talk to him.

Sam was standing next to her silently, not making eye contact with Tanner, but prepared to step in as best he could to protect his sister if needed. Tanner had nothing but respect for that.

"You ready for the camping trip next week?" he asked Eva. "You're going to have a great time."

Eva nodded vehemently, but her little face scrunched up as she pointed at the dog standing between her and Sam. "Mom says Tromso can't go."

Tanner reached down and petted the oversize pup named after the city in Norway where thousands of people flock every year to see the northern lights.

Since the pup's mom was named Corfu, after an island in Greece, the name sort of fit.

"Yeah, Tromso's not quite ready for that type of adventure yet. He might get into something poisonous or run off before we could grab him. Better let him stay here where he'll be nice and safe."

Eva considered him soberly. "That's probably true. Mom says Tromso can find trouble faster than anyone she's ever seen."

As if to make her point, the dog began pushing at Eva with his nose, wanting her to play. Eva giggled—a beautiful sound. Even Sam looked up and smiled when Tromso put his wet nose against the boy's stomach.

Eva let out a sigh. "Mom also says we've got to get all our schoolwork done or we can't go."

Tanner couldn't imagine any circumstances under which Marilyn wasn't going to allow her children to go on this beloved camping trip, but he didn't let that cat out of the bag. "You guys better work hard then. It would be a shame to miss it."

"Do you think Mr. Noah will come back this Saturday?" Sam asked softly, staring down and rubbing at some invisible stain in the carpet with his foot. "He and I were supposed to finish hanging the shower rod in the new bathroom."

"I'm sure he will," Tanner said, knowing that even if his brother had to break plans, he would be here if it meant Sam wouldn't be disappointed. Kid had already been let down too many times in his life.

Tanner's words seemed to be all the encouragement the children needed. They made a beeline back to the table with their work. Marilyn mouthed the words *thank you* to him. He just smiled.

Tanner waited as Bree finished her discussions with the other women, listening and commenting when they asked for his opinion. He loved how confident Bree had become since starting her position here. He could still remember the first night Cassandra had mentioned the possibility and how Bree had scoffed at the thought of being able to teach others. But now she was much more easily able to speak her mind and share her opinions, at least with small groups. She'd battled through her fears and had come out on the other side stronger for it.

He couldn't wait to make this woman his wife.

Holding her hand after dinner at the Sunrise Diner, Tanner walked her to her apartment on the outskirts of town. Most of her stuff was already at his ranch house—soon to be their house—on the land he shared with Noah. But neither of them trusted themselves to keep the no-sex agreement if they were both sleeping under the same roof. So Bree had been staying back at her apartment for the last two months.

He was definitely an idiot to have suggested the no-sex plan.

Bree sighed softly as they walked into her apartment. Tanner pulled her up against him.

"Please tell me that sigh means you're going to call me a moron for suggesting we not have sex until the wedding." He reached down and began nibbling at her lips. "Because I feel like that was the most stupid thing I've ever said in my entire life."

He rubbed up against her like a damned teenager. Bree smiled and wrapped her arms around his neck.

"No, this particular sigh was concerning Marilyn."

Tanner took a breath and forced himself to step back.

"About her position at New Journeys? I thought she was doing a good job."

She shook her head. "No, she's doing a wonderful job. Cassandra and I both know that neither of us could do as good a job as Marilyn is doing. She just mentioned that her husband might get out on bail. She's concerned for her and the kids."

Tanner couldn't blame the woman for that. "Because of the restraining order and the violence against her, she should be notified right away if her husband makes bail." He reached over and slid both his hands under Bree's hair on either side of her neck. "I've seen the police report for what happened to Marilyn. No judge is going to let him out on bail knowing what he tried to do."

"I just don't want anything to happen to her or the kids."

He pulled her closer and kissed her forehead. He loved her protectiveness of her friend. "Have I mentioned how excited I am to be marrying you in just a couple more weeks? Cass said you had some wedding stuff to deal with today. Did it go okay?"

"Yeah. Wedding dress fitting." She didn't sound too thrilled.

"I can't wait to see you in it." Bree's taste in cloth-

ing leaned toward casual. And as much as he loved it
when she stole one of his shirts to tie at her waist and
wear with her jeans—or even better, wore only his
shirt and *nothing* else—he was truly looking forward
to that first glance at her walking down the aisle.

She sighed. "Are you sure I can't talk you into
dragging me in front of the nearest judge like you
once threatened?"

"I'm pretty sure the women of this town, led by
my sister, would string up you and me both by our
toes if we eloped."

Bree laughed. The sound was soft and simple and
genuinely happy. He was looking forward to hearing
that sound for the next fifty years or so.

She chewed on her lip for just a moment, then
stepped a little closer, trailing one finger up his chest.
"Are you sure I can't talk you into going before a
judge tomorrow morning? You can outrun a bunch
of women. You're Captain Hot Lips."

Her own little hot lips pressed against his, her
tongue running against the seam of his mouth, before biting down gently with her teeth. "If we knew
we were getting married in front of the judge tomorrow," she continued, "there would be no reason for
us not to make love right here, right now, against this
wall. Doesn't that sound like the best plan ever?"

He could feel her smiling against his mouth as he
reached under her thighs and picked her up, trapping
her body between the wall and his torso. They both
let out a groan as her legs came around his hips and
brought them flush up against one another.

"There's nothing I want more than to peel you out of those clothes and spend the rest of the night making love to you on every available surface in this apartment," he growled into her mouth.

She let out a gasp as his lips found the side of her neck. It may have been two months since he'd last seen her naked, but he definitely remembered every single spot on her body that could drive her crazy.

"Then do it," she said. "I won't let the meanie town ladies hurt you. I just want to be married to you tomorrow."

Using every ounce of self-control he had, Tanner forced himself to ease Bree back down onto her feet and step away from her.

Two more weeks. He wanted to do this right. Wanted the next time they made love to be as husband and wife.

"We will get married. But in the church in front of all our family and friends, the way it should be. The way you deserve. I want everyone in this county— hell, the entire state—to know that you are who I very proudly choose as my wife. I don't want there to be any mistake about that, no rumored whispers that might accompany a quick trip to the judge."

She genuinely looked disappointed. "Fine."

He chuckled. "The wedding won't be as bad as you think."

"For you, maybe. You don't have to wear the scratchy white netting stuff."

"Tulle?"

"Damn it, how does everyone know the name of that material except me?"

He reached over and kissed her again. "You wear tulle for me for just a few hours and then you never have to wear it again."

"Promise?" she whispered.

"Absolutely. As a matter of fact, after we're married, I'm going to do my best to make sure you spend as much time as possible wearing nothing at all."

Chapter Three

Damn Tanner and his smooth talking. Five hours after he left, Bree still couldn't sleep.

Part of it was being wound up from their heavy make-out session against the wall. The other part was the fact that she hadn't been able to talk him into going before the judge, so those damn vows were still coming up and she had no idea what she was going to say.

I will love you forever and always my whole life, you and no one else.

Yeah, that was perfect.

If she was looking for complete stupidity meets *Braveheart.*

Bree punched the pillow beside her. Why were emotions so hard for her? Why did there seem to be so many variables that she had to take into consideration when writing these vows?

And why couldn't she get any sleep?

A few minutes later she finally just gave up and decided to go work in her office at the New Journeys building. Sitting at her own desk with her computer would at least be more familiar. And it had to be more useful than lying here tossing and turning in bed.

Twenty minutes later, dressed in a sweatshirt and yoga pants, she discovered that staring at a blank screen on her computer in her office was, in fact, just as bad as tossing and turning in bed.

She had nothing.

What the hell was she supposed to say to explain to the man she loved that she loved him?

Wasn't actually *getting married* enough of a declaration?

And the *tulle*? Wasn't tulle enough of a declaration of love, for heaven's sake? A solemn description of what agonies she was willing to bear for him?

When no other words or ideas came to her, she did the only thing she knew how to do: she opened her browser and began coding. Within fifteen minutes she had a program written that would automatically filter every mention of wedding vows from the internet and into a folder. She may not be able to write these vows herself but she could at least research—

She froze, head spinning to the side as something caught her peripheral vision on one of the black-and-white monitors on the table in the corner. What the heck was that?

Those monitors were set to the cameras recording the section of the building that hadn't been remodeled yet. Bree and Cassandra had installed them after some town teenagers were caught having a little rowdy fun back there. Bree had written a quick program that caused the cameras only to record if motion was detected.

Evidently motion had been detected.

Bree's fingers flew across the keyboard so she could bring up the footage on her computer monitor, which provided a much larger and clearer picture of the uninhabited area. Except the picture wasn't much clearer. It took her a moment to realize it wasn't because of a problem with her computer, but because the room was full of smoke.

The building was on fire.

Bree grabbed the phone on her desk and dialed 911.

"Grand County emergency services. You've reached 911. What's your emergency?"

"Debbie, it's Bree Daniels." Recognizing the 911 operator was definitely one of the perks of living in a small town. "There's a fire at New Journeys. Not in the main section, thank God, but it might spread. Send the fire trucks around to the back to the section that hasn't been renovated yet. I'm going to see if I can get it under control with the fire extinguisher."

"Now wait a minute, Bree. You need to stay on the line with me so we can direct the first responder—"

Bree didn't wait for Debbie to finish her sentence. The woman had lived in Risk Peak her whole life. She knew exactly where to send the first responders.

Bree grabbed the fire extinguisher in the corner of her office and dashed out into the hall, yanking down the fire alarm. Her office was on the opposite end of the housing area—uniquely situated between the residential space and the area that hadn't been renovated. Pulling the alarm would be the quickest way to get everyone out without having to run down to the living quarters herself.

Because maybe she could stop this whole thing before it got out of hand.

Once the alarm was blaring, she dashed back into her office and out the door on the other side that took her into the section of the building where the fire was located. She started in a sprint down the hall to the room where the motion had triggered the camera, but soon slowed. Already smoke was starting to fill the hallway.

The farther down the hall Bree went, the thicker the smoke became. Would she be able to put out a blaze making this much smoke with a single fire extinguisher? She had to try.

She heard some sort of screeching noise ahead of her and started to run again, coughing as she took in more smoke. Was somebody trapped back here? Teenagers fooling around again who accidentally started a fire and got trapped?

She turned the corner and dropped low in the thick smoke, crawling forward now. It almost sounded like someone was calling her name, but she couldn't tell from where. The smoke and her own coughing had her disoriented already, and that screeching noise was growing louder.

Someone had to be trapped in there. She pushed forward faster.

Extinguisher in one hand, she reached for the door

handle with the other and let out a shriek when an arm wrapped around her waist and lifted her off her knees, spinning her around.

"Oh, no you don't," a voice said in her ear. "You're not getting out of the tulle that easily."

"Tanner." His name came out in a relieved cough. "There's a fire. I heard a noise and I think someone was calling my name. It's behind that door."

"That was *me* calling your name. We've got to go."

She gestured toward the door. "But what about the noise? There may be someone trapped in there."

The screeching noise got higher and louder and Tanner muttered a curse under his breath, tucking his arm around her and launching her toward the corner. They just made it around and she was about to argue her case again when a thundering explosion roared from where they'd just been standing. Smoke encased the hall from top to bottom.

"What—" Bree stuttered.

"Too many accelerants in a construction area. It was like a pressure cooker."

A pressure cooker that would've killed her if Tanner hadn't been there to stop her from opening that door and get her out of the hallway.

Taking the fire extinguisher, he tucked her under his arm again and propelled them both back toward her office. Once there she was at least able to breathe again.

"You're going to have to let the firefighters go after

that blaze, freckles. There's nothing you can do. Let's just get everybody out of the front of the building."

She nodded, sucking in huge gulps of air. "You saved my life. I just called 911 a couple minutes ago. How did you get here so fast?"

"I was already here when you pulled the alarm."

They rushed together toward the housing units.

"You were? Why?"

He stopped for the briefest of seconds and gave her a hard kiss, before taking her arm and spurring her down the hall once again. "I went by your apartment to tell you I wanted *both*. We could go before the judge tomorrow *and* have the church wedding in two weeks. All I knew was I had to have you in bed with me tonight. When you weren't there, I came over here to plead my case."

"Holy hell," she whispered, then coughed again. "If you hadn't needed a booty call…"

She would've been dead.

He gave a short bark of laughter and shook his head grimly at the same time. "Yeah. Thank God I'm addicted to you."

A few moments later they were in the housing area.

"Bree!" Marilyn said. "What's going on? Is this some sort of drill?"

Bree was still coughing from the smoke she'd taken in and her run down both hallways.

"No," Tanner answered for her. "Not a drill. Everybody needs to get out. There's a fire in the other section of the building."

The panic was almost instantaneous. Mothers began calling for their children and some of the other women yelled for anyone who might still be asleep. Most of the kids were crying and Eva and Sam were looking up at Bree and Tanner, eyes huge in their pale faces, Tromso's leash in their hand.

Bree couldn't stop coughing. It paired horribly with the dog's whining.

Tanner put both hands on her shoulders. "You need to get outside and stop exerting yourself." He turned to Marilyn. "Can she take the kids outside and you and I will get everyone else out?"

Marilyn nodded.

Bree started to argue but another coughing fit overtook her. Tanner was right—he and Marilyn would get everyone out. The most she could do to help right now would be to get out of the way. She nodded and offered Eva and Sam her hands. They took them and she led them quickly outside, some of the other residents along with them.

Outside was pure chaos. Lights from fire trucks, police cars and ambulances lit up their block like it was some sort of disco rave party. Half the town was frantically pacing back and forth, and everyone seemed to be talking all at once.

Eva and Sam were looking even more traumatized, so Bree pulled them back toward the outer edge of the action. She wanted to reassure them, but every time she started talking she was besieged by coughs. So she just crouched beside them and put an arm around each small, shivering body.

It wasn't long before a paramedic came up to her.

"Miss, I think we ought to get your cough checked out. Can you come with me?"

She shook her head. She wasn't leaving Sam and Eva alone in this craziness. "I'll stay with them," she managed to get out.

The paramedic smiled at the kids. "Yeah, this is pretty nuts, isn't it?"

They both nodded solemnly.

He gave Bree a kind smile. "This sort of situation can be pretty overwhelming for folks their age, especially in the middle of the night. But you really ought to get that cough checked out. How about if I escort you over to the ambulance, and I'll personally stay with the kiddos to make sure they're not scared."

"I don't know—"

"I can keep them over at the side, out of harm's way and where it's not so chaotic. Probably best for everyone that way." He gave her a smile.

Bree was about to agree, but then she looked down at Sam and Eva, who still hadn't said a word. One silent tear rolled down Sam's cheek and he was clutching Tromso's leash with shaking fingers.

No. She wasn't leaving them. She didn't care if she had to hack up a lung until Tanner and Marilyn arrived.

"I'm fine. I'll stay with them," she whispered.

The paramedic looked like he was going to argue, but then there was some yelling closer to the building, so he shrugged and took off. Bree sat watching the burning building, clutching two tiny hands in hers, trying to establish the extent of the damage in the dark. And offering up constant prayers that no one had been hurt.

When Tanner jogged over to her a couple minutes later, she didn't resist at all as he pulled her against his chest. He smelled like smoke, but she was sure she smelled the same. "Everybody's out and accounted for. Doesn't look like anyone was hurt or that there was much damage to the living quarters."

Marilyn clutched her kids to her and they all watched the firefighters attack the blaze in the back of the building. It looked like most of it was contained back there, not the living quarters, but it was impossible to tell.

More townspeople continued to gather around. Tanner had to step up into his role of law enforcement when some teenagers kept trying to get too close to record for social media what was mostly now just smoke.

The blaze was completely out before Bree let Tanner lead her over to one of the ambulances so she could be examined. The younger, female paramedic was quite a bit less friendly than the guy Bree had met outside, stuffing an oxygen mask over Bree's face and suggesting she go to the hospital for follow-up. Bree didn't want to go but knew from the determined look in Tanner's eyes there would be a trip to get her lungs checked out in the next few hours. She might as well get it out of the way tonight.

Because it looked like there was going to be a whole lot of stuff requiring her attention tomorrow.

Chapter Four

Tanner had almost lost Bree.

Two days later that knowledge still wasn't ever very far out of his mind. If he'd gotten there one minute later, if he hadn't been thinking with his libido rather than his brain, she would've opened that door and provided the fire somewhere to escape.

And the escape would've been straight through her.

She hadn't been aware that the screeching noise they heard from inside the room was from the fire building in intensity. Opening the door would've provided more oxygen to the flames and caused them to engulf her.

If she'd opened that door, they would've been planning the final details of a funeral today rather than a wedding. Fear still clawed inside his gut at the thought, as he sat staring at the charred remains of the doorway.

"Pretty jarring to look at, isn't it?" Grand County fire inspector Randall Abrahams said from behind Tanner.

It would take a couple of days before the official

report would be filed and Tanner could act on it, so Randall had agreed to meet Tanner out here as a personal favor in order to try to get this wrapped up before the wedding.

"You have no idea. Bree almost opened that door."

Randall whistled through his teeth. "If she had, this definitely would've been a homicide investigation rather than plain old arson."

Tanner turned. "You're sure it was arson? There were a lot of building supplies and leftover stuff from the construction. Maybe not stored properly or something. An accident could've lit it on fire."

Randall walked around Tanner and entered the room where the blaze had started. "That was our initial thought."

"But something changed your mind." It wasn't a question.

"When we talked to your fiancée, we found out that she had put a security camera in here. That's how she realized the building was on fire so quickly—the camera turned on when the smoke and blaze got big enough to trigger the motion detector."

"Yes, that's right."

"Did you help rig that camera? Know anything about it?"

Tanner shook his head. "Not a whole lot. Cassandra and Bree wanted to do it themselves. I gave them a couple good camera suggestions and then looked it over once they had it hung. Seemed fine to me."

"But someone could've sneaked by the camera?"

"Yeah, definitely." Tanner shrugged, looking

around. "They were just trying to keep teenagers out of trouble, not provide full-fledged security for an empty section of the building."

"Camera was up in that corner, right?"

"Yes." Tanner took a step farther into the room with the older man, stepping carefully around the debris left by the fire and the hoses. "Do you think someone sneaked in around the camera and lit the fire? I checked the footage first thing and there was nothing. Just the blaze itself."

"Did you go back any further than the night of the fire?"

Tanner nodded, still looking around at the mess. "Yeah, just in case someone had been hiding in here. Nothing had triggered the camera in the forty-eight hours before the fire. The footage doesn't keep more than that."

"Let me show you what we found."

Randall and Tanner stepped carefully through the debris until they were standing in the corner of the room directly under where the camera had been located before it was destroyed in the fire.

"You're gonna have to tell me what you want me to see, because it all looks like the bottom of my fire pit to me," Tanner told him.

Randall pulled out a plastic evidence bag from his pocket. "This is what I want you to see, and this corner was where we found it."

Tanner took the bag, squinting at it as he held it up. Randall didn't keep him in suspense.

"It's a timer. We found parts of it and a pretty sophisticated detonation device in this corner. Somebody very definitely set this fire."

Tanner let out a low curse. "A sophisticated detonator goes well beyond some kids playing a prank or a firebug who wanted to watch a building burn."

"I agree. This was set with deliberate intent to go off exactly when it did. And I think someone broke in here ahead of time and planted the device and timer. It could've been a while ago, but every day it sat here, it risked detection."

Tanner ran a hand through his hair. "So it was probably in the last couple of days. And if there's no record of it in the footage, that means whoever sneaked in here knew where that camera was located and how to avoid it."

This had just become much more serious than any of them had counted on.

Tanner studied the evidence bag and its contents. "But to what end? Were they trying to blow up the whole building? Kill everyone?"

Randall shook his head. "No. If anything, the opposite. I know Bree was here and called the fire department much more quickly than would've occurred on any other night. But the way this fire was set up, it would've burned itself out before it ever got to the inhabited side of the building. I don't think it was meant to harm anyone."

"Well, it damn nearly harmed Bree."

Randall gave an apologetic shrug. "That's true, but on any other given night she wouldn't have been here."

"So, we are looking at some sort of explosives expert?"

What the hell would one be doing at a women's shelter? Especially if they weren't trying to blow the building up? This didn't make a lot of sense.

"Not necessarily. Yes, an explosives expert would know how to do all of this and it's definitely beyond what your normal amateur pyromaniac is involved with. But there are certain jobs—military, construction, even some welding jobs—that would also provide that sort of knowledge. Or it could be hired out."

"I liked this much better when I thought it might be a run-of-the-mill arsonist just trying to burn the place down. Now we're talking about someone with a specific skill set who also has studied New Journeys enough to know the basics about their security and what would or wouldn't happen in a fire."

"I don't blame you there. A pyro may be a pain in the ass, but they're also predictable. Their endgame is to watch the world burn."

Tanner looked around, trying to put himself in the arsonist's mind. "What was this guy's endgame? No one was hurt. Nothing was stolen, as far as we know."

Randall walked over and slapped him on the shoulder. "That, my friend, is your job and thankfully not mine."

Randall showed Tanner a few more things, including where the fire would've burned out on its own if the fire department hadn't stopped it before that. And he was right—it definitely wouldn't have hurt anyone, unless, like Bree, they just happened to be wandering in that section of the building.

As Tanner walked back to his office, he kept trying to figure out what the motive was.

What was the purpose? That was the ultimate question. All this had really served to do was shake everyone up.

He let out a low curse. Maybe that was the purpose—getting everyone shaken up. Thanks to the fire, everyone was back in the old building where there was much less security and no set routine.

Ronnie Kitchens, the other deputy in their office, met Tanner as soon as he walked in the door. "That face doesn't look good. Problems?"

Tanner explained about the detonator and everything else Randall had told him.

Ronnie let out a low whistle. "That's not good."

"The only people I can think that might have something to gain from pulling a stunt like this would be the men involved in these women's lives."

"Definitely. Although I would think they'd want to do as much damage as possible, not set a blaze that would burn out on its own. The residents will be able to move back in in just a couple more days."

They walked toward Tanner's office. "Maybe the plan is to make the women not feel safe at New Journeys so they'll be more likely to return to their previous situations."

That was a common enough problem under the

best of circumstances for some of these women; it wouldn't take much to encourage them to leave.

"Pull the files we started on all the men connected to the current residents at New Journeys. We need to cross-reference them with their backgrounds and professions. We're looking for anyone with a military background or who has worked in construction, demolition or anything that would provide training in explosives."

Ronnie began the cross-referencing while Tanner put a call in to Cassandra. He didn't want to cause any undue panic, but he wanted his sister and Bree to be aware of the situation. He promised to call them back if he had any solid suspects.

Three frustrating hours later, despite working through lunch, they hadn't found any promising suspects. The two men who seemed most *qualified* to have set the fire both lived out of state. Phone calls to their current places of employment had provided solid alibis. There was no way they could've been at work all week across the country and then made it to Risk Peak and back.

The couple of others who might have the knowledge were in prison, including Jared Ellis, Marilyn's husband, who worked in construction.

Ronnie sat back in the chair across from Tanner's desk, two files balancing on his leg crossed at the knee. "If our perp isn't someone associated with New Journeys, could it be someone coming after Bree? She was the only one who had to be taken to the hospital. Granted, most of the Organization is behind bars, but after what happened in Atlanta—"

Ronnie was about to say something else when the phone on Tanner's desk rang.

"Hold that thought." Although there damn well better not be anyone coming after Bree again. He picked up the phone. "Tanner Dempsey speaking."

"Captain Dempsey, this is Conrad Parnam with the Denver County Warrants and Bonding Office." The man's voice was sort of distant and breathy, like the phone wasn't directly next to his mouth. Or like he was bored with the conversation before it even started.

"What can I do for you, Mr. Parnam?"

"I'm trying to reach a Mrs. Marilyn Ellis at a facility called New Journeys but I'm having difficulty. Do you have a way to get in touch with her?"

"I do." He had a sinking suspicion he knew where this was going and wasn't going to like it.

"Because of the restraining order against Mrs. Ellis's husband, Jared Ellis, we wanted to let her know that he was released on bail."

Yep, he didn't like it. This already bad day just got worse. "Earlier today?"

He could hear Parnam shuffling through papers. "Actually, no. Mr. Ellis was released three days ago."

Chapter Five

Tanner fought not to roar into the phone. Jared Ellis was released from a Denver county jail *three* days ago and no one had told Marilyn?

He forced himself to speak reasonably, even though he had a white-knuckled grip on the phone. "Three days ago? Why wasn't Mrs. Ellis notified immediately? Jared Ellis is considered to be a threat to both her and her children."

"You know how it is. Things sometimes fall through the cracks." There was no apology in Parnam's tone.

Tanner wrote the word *Noah* on the notepad and spun it around so Ronnie could see it. Ronnie nodded and Tanner tapped the phone in his hand to indicate Ronnie needed to tell Noah about Jared Ellis's release. Ronnie already had his phone in hand as he walked out of the office.

This was definitely a police matter, but when it came to protecting Marilyn and those kids, it was a personal matter also. Noah would want to know.

"I'm going to need the details about Ellis's release," he said into the phone.

"Is there some sort of problem?" Finally something else took the place of boredom in Parnam's tone: irritation. But Tanner didn't give a damn if Parnam was perturbed that he would have to actually do his job.

"Yes, there's a problem. We have a woman in our care here who was damn near beaten to death by her husband. So finding out he's been out on bail for three days and nobody saw fit to notify either her or my office is very much a problem."

"Look, I just run the paperwork for whoever the judge tells me to and make the calls that come across my desk. Nothing more or less than that. But hang on a minute and let me see what I can find out." Irritation still painted the other man's tone, but at least Tanner could hear the clicking of his fingers on the keyboard. "Judge doesn't usually let violent offenders out on bail." More clicking. "Well, that explains it. Oscar Stobbart. He's a very high-end defense attorney—has a great record of getting people out on bail, and honestly, getting them reduced sentencing. Ellis must have a ton of money to hire someone like him."

Tanner was now frustrated with himself that he didn't know more about Jared Ellis. But he honestly hadn't thought there would be much he needed to know since the man was behind bars. Did he have money? Tanner didn't know.

But he was out. And more important, had been out of jail within the window for setting the detonator for the fire. "Do you at least have his last known address?" They would definitely be paying a visit to Jared as soon as possible.

"Actually, I can do a little better than an address. As part of Mr. Ellis's bail, he was placed on a GPS tracking monitor. That was probably why it wasn't a priority for me to call Mrs. Ellis or your office. Jared Ellis is required to stay within a two-mile radius of his listed home address, which is in downtown Denver."

An ankle monitor was good news. "So you can tell where he's been at any particular hour? What happens if he leaves the two-mile radius?"

"Yep, there's a log that keeps record of exactly where he is at any given time. And if Ellis leaves the radius for which the monitor is set, it automatically sets up an alarm with the Denver marshals. They'll be at his house in minutes. Plus, it's completely unhackable."

"So if I wanted to know where he was two nights ago, you could get that for me." If there was some sort of glitch in this "unhackable" system, Tanner wanted to know about it.

Parnam gave a long-suffering sigh. "How about if I just send you the entire log of Ellis's whereabouts since the moment he was released. That will save us a number of different calls and emails, don't you think?"

And would require a lot less work from Parnam.

"Fine. I'll expect it in an email within the next hour."

Tanner hung up without waiting for a response.

The fact that Ellis had been released without notifying Marilyn would be addressed within the system.

But right now, until they could confirm *exactly* where Jared Ellis was, he needed to get security on Marilyn and her kids.

He had Ronnie start the paperwork for protective surveillance, even though Tanner knew the approval was a long shot unless a direct threat to Marilyn and the kids could be proved—which hopefully it would be as soon as they checked Ellis's whereabouts on the night of the fire.

He was also going to request the live data from Parnam's office. Knowing where Jared *had been* afterward wasn't good enough. They needed to know his current whereabouts. Not that Tanner didn't trust the Denver marshal's office to do their job. But all it would take was Jared tricking the system *one time* and he could attack Marilyn. And as long as that was a possibility—until Jared's trial when he went away long-term—Tanner wanted to be multiple steps ahead of the other man.

Right now that included making sure Marilyn knew her ex was out of jail.

His cell phone buzzed on his belt with a call from Noah before Tanner even made it out of the office.

"Ronnie said Jared Ellis was released on bail?" His brother didn't even waste time with a greeting.

Neither did Tanner. "Affirmative."

Noah's curse was foul. "Does the sheriff's office have money to put surveillance on Marilyn and the kids?"

"I've already got the process started, but I'll be honest, unless we get proof that Ellis is a threat to her or was anywhere in the area of the fire, then I don't have much of a legal leg to stand on."

"I'm on my way into town. If we can't get a uniform on her, then I'll take up watch duty myself. It's very suspicious that there was a fire at New Journeys at the same time Ellis got out on bail."

Tanner began walking down the block toward the old New Journeys building. It would be quicker than driving. "Especially since it looks like someone started it deliberately." He explained what the fire inspector had found.

Noah cursed again.

"I've spent all day trying to figure out why someone would've started a fire that wasn't trying to hurt anyone or burn down the building," Tanner said.

"It might have made a perfect opportunity for Jared to snatch Marilyn and the kids. Probably wouldn't have taken into account how much the people of Risk Peak would be surrounding them."

"Definitely true," Tanner said. "Although the fire may have nothing to do with Ellis."

"I'm not willing to take that chance," Noah said quietly. "Or take the chance that he's just going to leave Marilyn alone. She's been through enough."

They both felt that way. It was the very reason he'd had Ronnie call his brother to begin with. "I'll meet you at the old New Journeys building."

Even though there hadn't been much damage to the living quarters of the new building by the fire, they'd still moved everyone back into the old building while the initial cleaning was going on. Tanner wasn't thrilled about the change. It definitely didn't have the security upgrades the new building had.

When he arrived at New Journeys' current home, he immediately asked to talk to Marilyn. He hated to see the shadows cross the quiet woman's face when she saw him. She knew this was going to be bad news.

Bree was there and gave him a tight smile. "I'll just hang out in the office so you two can talk. Give you guys some privacy."

Tanner nodded, but Marilyn shook her head, holding her hand out to Bree. "No, stay. This is going to affect all of us. The kids are doing schoolwork, so this is a good time. Let's go into the kitchen."

Bree reached over and grabbed Tanner's hand as Marilyn put on a pot of coffee with jerky movements.

"Do you want to bring Cassandra in too?" Tanner asked.

Bree shook her head. "She's not here. She's having a throwdown with the insurance company, trying to get us back in the other building by next week. But evidently she's having some difficulties because of what's in the fire report."

Tanner nodded. "The fire inspector thinks the blaze was deliberate." He turned back to Marilyn, who was trying to pour the coffee she'd made with shaky hands. Damn it, he didn't want to have this conversation. He tried to start but couldn't force the words out.

"Just tell me," Marilyn said softly, when she

handed him his mug. "It's Jared, right? He made bail?"

Bree muttered a curse that would've made Cassandra proud.

Tanner nodded.

"Yes. Three days ago."

Nope, *this* new string of curses from Bree would've made Cassandra proud.

Marilyn blanched. "Three days ago? I thought they were going to tell me immediately if he made bail."

It was so hard to watch Marilyn's sense of safety and security be torn away with his words. The skin across her cheekbones was drawn and pale. Her shoulders hunched in as if to protect herself from a blow.

"I know. They should have told you right away. It was some sort of communication breakdown, but it was wrong and I'm very sorry."

Marilyn was clutching her coffee like a drowning victim would a lifeline.

"But there is a little bit of good news," Tanner continued. "Jared is on an ankle tracker. I've got the Denver County bonding office sending me the log for everywhere Jared has been since the moment he got out. I've also got one of my men looking into seeing if we can get direct access to the live data, so we know where he is at all times."

"I thought you said Jared wouldn't get out on bail given what he did," Bree said softly.

He grimaced. "Yeah, I'll be honest, I was shocked

to hear it. Evidently he got himself one of the most expensive and well-connected lawyers in the state."

"Jared has a lot of powerful friends. His fraternity brothers," Marilyn whispered.

"Is Oscar Stobbart one of those?" Tanner asked.

If possible, Marilyn's face got even whiter. "Yes."

There was a wealth of agony in that single word. Tanner didn't press, but he could imagine that there was probably a lot more to Marilyn's abuse than she had let anyone know about.

A soft tap at the kitchen door had them all turning in that direction. It was Noah.

"I asked Noah to come by just for added security until we have a true grip on what's going on. Is that okay?" Tanner said. The last thing either he or Noah wanted was to make Marilyn more uncomfortable.

Marilyn was staring at Noah through the glass panes of the kitchen door. She nodded. "No, I'll feel better if he's here."

Noah never took his eyes from Marilyn as he walked in the door. He didn't move near her, but his focus and awareness of her were almost tangible.

"You can do this," he said softly.

Marilyn didn't look like she believed him, but she just shrugged and said, "Doesn't look like I have any choice." She rubbed a hand across her eyes. "I should probably leave. Take the kids and get farther away."

"No," Noah said. "He's not going to get to you."

His brother's volume might be soft and his tone even, but there was no way to mistake the certainty behind the words. For the first time since Tanner arrived, Marilyn relaxed just the slightest bit. She probably didn't even know about Noah's background in Special Forces. But when Noah gave his word that he was going to protect her, he had the skills to back up that promise.

Noah Dempsey may be a rancher by trade, but that didn't change the fact that he was also a warrior in every possible way.

"If Jared got out on bail three days ago, could he have been the one who set the fire?" Marilyn asked.

Tanner glanced over at Noah, then at Marilyn. "We don't know for sure, but if Jared was involved, it would answer a lot of questions."

"Like what?" Bree asked.

Noah leaned back against the counter. The women didn't recognize the stance for what it was, but Tanner did. Noah was placing himself between Marilyn and any danger that might come through that door.

Tanner took a sip of his coffee. "It looks like the fire was set deliberately, but whoever did it wasn't trying to burn the building down completely or even hurt anyone."

"It was set to shake things up," Noah said. "Get everyone out of their routine."

"They certainly managed that," Bree muttered.

"He could've been out there," Marilyn whispered. "Waiting to get me or the kids alone. That's exactly something Jared would do."

"And none of us suspected there was any danger." Bree shook her head. "I almost left the kids with a paramedic. He wouldn't have known to look out for Jared."

Tanner rubbed the back of his neck. "We can't automatically assume it was Jared. He's got that ankle monitor, and it sends a notification if he goes out of his set range. My colleague in Denver assures me it isn't hackable."

Bree actually laughed out loud, rolling her eyes. "Okay. We'll just let them go on believing that. *Everything* is hackable."

He reached over and grabbed his little computer genius's hand. "Everything is hackable by *you*. The chances that Jared has someone with your skill in his personal list of friends—no matter how many fraternity brothers he has—is slim."

Bree nodded. "Agreed. All I'm saying is that a false sense of security that something can't be hacked might lead to laziness on law enforcement's part."

Tanner couldn't disagree with that. Not when the department already didn't have a stellar showing when it came to this situation.

A text came in on his phone from Ronnie. Finally a little good news.

"Ronnie got the log for Jared's monitor. According to the reports, he was not anywhere around Risk Peak at the time of the fire. He hasn't been out of Denver city limits since he made bail."

"Unless he did have someone who could hack the anklet for him," Bree said.

"Could you tell if it had been tampered with?"

Tanner asked her. "Would you be able to see if the reports of his whereabouts were wrong?"

"From the source computer or the anklet itself, yes," she said.

"Then maybe it's time you and I took a little field trip. A nice tour of the Denver County Warrants and Bonding Office seems like a great idea."

Chapter Six

"You let me do the talking, okay?"

Bree rolled her eyes. "Remember how for as long you've known me, I've never had any sort of desire to talk to people? Still true."

It was the next morning and Bree and Tanner were on their way to the Denver County Warrants and Bonding Office. Tanner had wanted to come yesterday, but by four o'clock the person they'd needed to see was already gone, he'd found out with disgust.

But it was better they made the trip today, since it had given Bree time to research the monitoring system being used on Jared. She had to admit, this one was sophisticated—definitely high-end. Most types of ankle monitors were meant for nonviolent first-time offenders—people who needed to be scared into staying in one place and were a pretty low flight risk overall. Those units were pretty easily hackable and would've definitely been a mistake in Jared's case.

But this version of electronic monitoring was much more advanced. Had been used successfully all over the country without anyone being able to escape undetected.

Regardless, Bree wanted to check out this system for herself. Wanted to know for certain Marilyn and the kids were safe. The easiest way to do that was through official access at the bonding office.

Of course, she could've hacked the system *without* official access, but she didn't even bring that possibility up. For some absurd reason, her law enforcement husband-to-be didn't like breaking the law. Go figure.

"I'm not going to explain to them outright what we're doing unless I have to," Tanner said. "Parnam didn't seem like a bad guy, but he definitely isn't interested in adding to his workload. Nobody in the warrants and bonding office is going to like us peeking over their shoulder to double-check their work. So let's try not to inform them."

Bree let out a frustrated sigh. "And what about Marilyn and the kids? Do they care at all that if Jared has found some way to circumvent the monitoring system, he might put Marilyn back in the hospital or worse?"

"As far as the law is concerned, Marilyn is protected because she has that restraining order."

"That restraining order isn't worth the paper it's printed on if Jared decides he's willing to risk getting away with it."

Tanner's long fingers wrapped around hers where her hand rested on her legs. "I agree, and that's why we've got Noah on the lookout. Ronnie has also volunteered to do some lookout shifts during his time off, and when Richard Whitaker heard about it, he offered also."

She had to smile at Whitaker's name. "How is our old friend the jackass?"

"He's coming to the wedding, you know."

The other officer was Tanner's counterpoint in the northern section of the county. He'd accused both Bree and Tanner of murder last year, but then had helped take care of Bree when Tanner had been near death in the hospital.

"I'm glad Marilyn will have protection," she said. "But we both know these are temporary measures."

"Just because Jared's lawyer managed to convince a judge that he's not a flight risk doesn't mean that he's not going to go to jail for a long time for what he did to her. I've seen the evidence. So even if we have to take turns watching over her and the kids for the next four months until the trial, we'll do it. Everyone is willing to help her out in that way."

She squeezed his hand, her heart filling up almost painfully with the emotions she felt for him. He was such a good man. Willing to do whatever he had to do to make sure the people who depended on him were safe.

"Thank you," she whispered, wishing she was better with words. Better at expressing everything she felt inside herself for him.

He brought her hand to his lips. "Marilyn and those kids deserve a fresh start. A future that doesn't involve pain or fear. All of us want to give them that."

"I do too." And she was going to do whatever she had to do to get the information she needed from that computer. If she could prove that Jared had been around Risk Peak during the fire—hell, *anytime* since he'd been released—he'd be spending the rest of his time awaiting trial behind bars.

Where he belonged.

They pulled up at the bonding office, attached to the courthouse and Denver marshals' office.

"I'm just going to introduce you as a computer expert," Tanner said as they got out of the vehicle. "I don't think anyone around here knows either of us, so introducing you as my colleague shouldn't raise any eyebrows."

She gave a brisk nod. "IT colleague here to help make sure that data is running smoothly between two different systems. Got it. Piece of cake."

They signed in at the front desk and made their way up a single flight of stairs to Parnam's office. The door was half open and Parnam, a pudgy man in his midfifties, an office phone lodged between his shoulder and jaw, gestured for them to come in. His voice was a blend of boredom and exhaustion as he read a series of numbers to whoever was on the phone.

Bree and Tanner took seats across from his desk as he hung up.

"Mr. Parnam, I'm Tanner Dempsey. This is IT expert Ms. Daniels."

Bree noticed how adeptly Tanner avoided lying.

Kept it just general enough to avoid telling any un-truths. Bree was an IT expert, after all.

"Dempsey. Ms. Daniels." Parnam nodded his head at both of them. "I've already sent you all the reports I have on Jared Ellis. I looked into the case a little myself, and I really am sorry Mrs. Ellis wasn't noti-fied. We had two people retire in the last six months and their positions haven't been backfilled, so, like I said, things just sometimes slip through the cracks."

Tanner raised an eyebrow. "I'm sorry to hear you're trying to work three people's jobs, because in a situation like this, Mrs. Ellis could've been hurt or worse, not even knowing there was any possible danger out there."

Parnam settled his weight back in his chair. "Well, in my defense, Ellis does have the ankle monitor on. If he had gone anywhere near his wife, it would've set off all sorts of alarms. That thing is unhackable."

Bree got straighter in her chair, trying to swal-low the words bubbling up her throat at his utter faith in technology. She'd spent most of her child-hood within an organization that made it their mis-sion in life to hack information systems and use it to their advantage.

Nothing was unhackable.

Next to her, Tanner cleared his throat. His fingers, resting on his knees, made a swiping gesture over and over. She got the message: don't do anything stupid like argue with Parnam. She forced herself to relax in the chair.

"Be that as it may," Tanner said. "Ms. Daniels is

here to make sure there won't be any problem with the data communicating between the Denver County and Grand County systems."

"Whatever." Parnam let out a weary sigh. "What do you need?"

"Ten minutes on the monitoring system," Bree responded. "I've already made sure our system is ready. I just need to double-check a couple of things in your system."

Parnam nodded and escorted Bree and Tanner to a separate office that contained a computer, a worktable with miscellaneous electronic equipment and sensors, and a couple of hard plastic chairs.

"This is where everything is calibrated and connected. Every offender to be fitted with a monitor comes in here, and those with the particular version being used for Jared Ellis come back once a week to make sure the calibration is still correct and the GPS system is online."

"But Ellis hasn't been back yet, right? He's not scheduled for a few more days?" Tanner asked.

"Actually, the tech should've had him in this morning. I put in the request since there was such concern from Grand County—I wanted to cover our bases. I haven't heard about any results yet, though. Those would go straight to the Denver marshals. Once I set up the initial paperwork, I'm pretty much out of the loop. If someone does go outside of their monitor's set parameters, the call goes to the Denver marshals, with a backup call to the Denver sheriff's departments. But their offices are here in the same building, so I usually hear about it."

"You don't work for the sheriff's department?" Bree asked.

"Parnam is a state employee, not law enforcement," Tanner said.

"Exactly. I'm just in charge of paperwork. I don't make the decision on who goes free or not—that's the judge. I don't chase down the people who decide to hammer off their anklet—that's the cops. I'm just trying to make sure everything gets filed correctly."

And the dude did not sound very excited about his job—not that Bree blamed him.

"So just go ahead and do what you need to do. You said it would only take a few minutes?" Parnam leaned up against the doorway.

She doubted he would know enough about computers to understand what she was going to do, but it would be a lot more complicated with him looking over her shoulder the whole time. She glanced over at Tanner, who gave her a brief nod.

Tanner put his hand on Parnam's shoulder. "Conrad, you probably don't get told this a lot, and that's a shame. But your job is very important. Just think of how long it would've taken for Mrs. Ellis to be notified that Jared had been released if it wasn't for you. I appreciate your hard work."

Bree sat down at the computer and managed not to roll her eyes. Tanner. That man could be the epitome of fierce warrior when the need called for it. She'd seen that herself when he'd fought to save their lives a few months ago. He'd been nearly dead—covered in his own blood from multiple gunshot wounds—and still managed to save them both.

But damned if he couldn't also charm his way out of most situations. He was just so *likable*. Parnam wasn't immune to Tanner's charm either.

"Thank you for saying that," the other man said. "I hear plenty if something goes wrong, but nobody ever thinks to say thank you for things going right."

Tanner made a sound of agreement and cleared his throat. "Well, we are thankful that you've done your job so well." Bree kept her eyes glued on the computer so she wouldn't snicker. "Would you mind showing me the way to the marshals' offices? I want to make sure that they understand the severity of the situation too, like you do."

"Yeah, absolutely." She wasn't surprised to hear that Parnam wanted to show Tanner, his new bestie, anything he needed to see. "Will you be okay in here by yourself, Ms. Daniels?"

Bree looked over her shoulder at them and smiled. "Absolutely. It will probably be much quicker for me without you two."

The two were chatting like pals as they walked down the hallway.

She didn't waste any time accessing the system and familiarizing herself with its particulars in just a few minutes. She immediately brought up the file on Jared's ankle monitor and pored over the data. It was identical to the report Tanner had shown her this morning, the same one that had been sent over by Parnam yesterday.

Of course, that didn't mean the anklet system hadn't been tampered with, just that Parnam probably wasn't in on it.

Closing down the tracking system, she opened a source-code editor and quickly coded a program she'd already developed in her mind, bootstrapping it so it could run immediately. The program was simple but powerful. It would determine whether any outside shells were attempting to hide the real data concerning Jared.

She was almost disappointed when it came back with nothing.

Closing that, she wrote another quick program— the coding coming easier to her than conversation would to most normal people—to look for GPS manipulation. That was pretty high-level, and she'd be impressed if Jared had somebody savvy enough to know how to reconfigure data based on that.

It was how she would do it.

But after a few more minutes it became clear no one had hacked Jared's monitoring system through that method either.

She tried the half dozen other ways she could think of to infiltrate the monitoring system but was either shut down by the system itself or found no evidence that the system had been tampered with in any way.

Finally, she just sat back and stared at the screen

in front of her, having to come to grips with what the data was telling her. Jared was clean.

She closed her source code and compiling windows and pulled up Jared's file again, staring at his picture. There was no doubt he was a handsome guy. Midthirties, blondish-brown hair, piercing blue eyes. A charming smirk, even in his mug shot.

"How did you do it, you bastard?"

His picture didn't respond.

She reopened her windows and wrote another program quickly to see if Jared might have just delayed the transmission of data in some way. That would've been pretty clever also. By the time the police realized they'd been fooled, he could've done all sorts of damage to Marilyn and the kids.

But that came back negative also.

Bree sat back, feeling something she didn't often at a computer: stumped.

Was it possible Jared didn't have anything to do with the fire at all? That perhaps he really had stayed within the two-mile radius he was allowed to travel in since his release? Because Bree was one of the top computer geniuses on the planet, and if he was fooling the system, then she couldn't figure out how it was being done.

The office door crashing open had her jumping in her seat. She immediately tapped the required keys to hide what she'd been doing, expecting to find Tanner returning with Parnam.

But instead it was Jared Ellis himself.

Chapter Seven

Jared was bigger than Bree would've thought. She imagined Marilyn, who was probably a good three inches shorter than Bree's own five foot five, struggling against him. It was hard to visualize a situation in which Marilyn would come out the victor.

A man stepped from behind Jared, much shorter, but still stocky. "This is pretty much harassment," the shorter man said in a booming voice. "My client has been out on bail for four days and we're already being called in here like he's done something wrong? Do not doubt I'm going to make sure the judge hears about this."

"I thought you came in earlier?" Bree said without thinking. Wasn't that what Parnam had said?

"Believe it or not, my client does not jump at the whims of this office. If the judge tells us to come in at a certain time, we will certainly comply, but this office having technical difficulties is not Mr. Ellis's problem. You're lucky he's here at all."

They didn't know who she was, of course. They

thought she was a computer tech assigned to this office.

This was a gift horse. She was going to ride that sucker, not look it in the mouth.

"Of course, Mr. Stobbart." Bree forced her most subdued tone. Wait—would the tech have known his name? Too late now. "We appreciate you and Mr. Ellis coming in so we can take a look at the hardware."

Stobbart looked slightly appeased, at least enough to stop yelling. "Well, I certainly wasn't going to allow my client here without representation," he huffed. "It's not my first day being a lawyer."

He and Jared both chuckled.

"If you don't mind stepping over here, I'll evaluate the hardware." She studied Jared's face. Stobbart may be a loud bully, but it was the look in Jared's eye that had her recoiling.

Jared Ellis was evil.

He hadn't said a word yet, and he didn't say a word now; he just walked over and placed his leg on the chair next to Bree's, exposing his ankle under his khaki pants. She wasn't surprised to find him wearing loafers.

If wearing loafers in Colorado didn't tell you everything you needed to know about a man, she didn't know what would.

"Have you attempted to remove the device or modify it in any way?" she asked. "Maybe it got uncomfortable so you did something to it?"

"Like what?" His voice was deep and low and had almost a hiss-like quality to it.

She yanked her gaze from his face and studied the ankle monitor. There were no scratches, no markings whatsoever to indicate it had been tampered with.

"Just any attempt to open the device. Believe it or not, some people could start to feel claustrophobic because they can't remove the hardware."

She had no idea if that was true, but it sounded reasonable enough.

"No. I'm not prone to claustrophobia." Icy voice once again.

There were no markings to indicate it had been overloaded with electricity, another way of attempting to dismantle it, but that would also have telltale signs.

"I'm just going to run a system diagnostics test while you're here," Bree said. "You shouldn't feel anything."

Although if she could've managed to rewrite the system so that the ankle monitor gave off a shock to Jared, she wouldn't have hesitated to do so. Unfortunately, the device didn't work that way.

She backdoored into the system, praying neither Jared nor his lawyer would understand what she was doing, and ran a full diagnostics test on everything: the monitor, the link between it and the system, the system itself.

She also made sure the GPS tracking was accurately calibrated, since she knew exactly where Jared was and could tell if it had been tampered with.

The system was perfect. The anklet was broadcasting exactly as it was meant to. Damn it.

She tried to think of any other tests she could run, but there wasn't anything. She was grasping at straws. She stared at the hardware, willing an idea to come to her.

"Are we done here? My client hasn't done anything wrong. Obviously the judge believes that to be true enough to release him on bail. I'm confident that Mr. Ellis will also be exonerated at his trial. We feel very certain of that. He'll be free of your technology soon enough."

Bree breathed past the bile pooling in her gut at the thought that this man could walk totally free. That Stobbart seemed so damn certain he would be. Jared just calmly rolled his pants leg back down, without a concern in the world.

"I hope you rot in hell." As soon as the impulsive whisper was out of her mouth, she wished she could take the words back. Then prayed she'd said it low enough that neither of them heard her.

She wasn't so lucky.

Jared's eyes narrowed into slits. "You know Marilyn, don't you?"

Bree scrambled out of her chair and backed up as Jared yanked his foot down and closed in on her. "Is she here? Where is she? I just want to talk to her."

"Jared, not here—" Stobbart grabbed his shoulder, but Jared shook him off.

"Stay the hell out of this, Oscar," Jared bit out, grabbing Bree by the upper arms and squeezing with bruising force. "You will tell me where my wife and family are. She's my *wife*. I have a right to see her. To explain my side of things."

Almost from a distance she heard the office door open and Tanner's angry roar over Jared's words. A second later Jared's painful fingers released her as he was thrown up against the wall by Tanner.

"What's going on here?" Parnam asked from the far side of the room, obviously not wanting to step in between Tanner and Jared.

"I'll tell you what's going on here…police brutality," Stobbart said.

But Tanner had already released Jared and was standing by Bree, keeping himself between her and the other man.

"Your client was manhandling and intimidating my colleague," Tanner said. "If you're looking for brutality, it was coming at the hands of your client."

"She knows where my wife is," Jared spit out. "I just want to talk to Marilyn."

"Jared, enough," Oscar said. "Think about long term."

"But she—"

"Enough!" Oscar yelled.

The room fell into silence except for Jared's breathing as he attempted to get himself under control.

"The only thing you need to know about your wife and kids is that the restraining order against you still stands. If you come anywhere near them, you're going right back to jail." Tanner looked over his shoulder at Bree. "Are you okay? Did you get what you needed?"

"Yes." She would have to give him the bad news later.

Stobbart was pulling Jared toward the door. "You can believe that this is all going to come back up in court. I'm not going to allow this to go unreported. My client has rights."

Tanner shook his head. "Your client is the worst kind of scum, and I'll look forward to making that fact known to anyone you want to bring this up with, judge included. There's nothing I'd like better."

Bree grabbed the back of his shirt, a little turned on by what a badass Tanner was. But mostly she just wanted them to get out of here.

Jared had regained his composure. "I'm okay, Oscar."

Oscar turned to Parnam. "I assume you've got all you needed for the device to be calibrated and my client won't be harassed again? We will only come in from now on if we're instructed to by the judge."

Parnam was still looking around trying to figure out exactly what was going on. "I guess so."

"Then let's go," Stobbart said to Jared, taking him by the arm.

Both men walked toward the office door, but Jared turned around just before they left. He looked straight at Bree with those icy eyes.

"I'm sure we'll be seeing each other again."

Tanner kept her body pinned all the way behind

his. She wouldn't even be able to see Jared if she didn't peek her head out from around Tanner's broad shoulders. She tried to step around him, to confront Jared herself, but Tanner wouldn't let her.

That was fine. She didn't really want to be face-to-face with Jared anyway. Not because she was afraid of him, but because she wasn't sure she could stop herself from punching him in the jaw—and that would just make Stobbart giddy with all the harassment suits he could file. So she stayed behind Tanner.

Jared and Stobbart left without another word.

Tanner immediately turned around and yanked her to his chest. "Are you sure you're all right? Did he hurt you?"

"Yes, I'm fine. Do you really think he doesn't know where Marilyn is?"

"I don't know. She's not announcing where she is, but she's not hiding it either. Jared is smart. It's a good way of professing his innocence without overtly drawing attention to it. But it's possible he doesn't know, I guess."

"What exactly is going on here?" Parnam asked, studying them.

Bree pulled away and they both turned back to Parnam. "Nothing has changed," Tanner said. "We're still trying to make sure Jared Ellis is not able to get anywhere near his wife, whom he assaulted bad enough to put into the hospital a few months ago."

Parnam nodded, then looked at Bree. "But you know his wife? I thought you worked for Grand County?"

"She's an independent contractor," Tanner said. Bree just nodded.

Parnam raised an eyebrow. "Fine. I don't want to get caught in the middle of anything. Somebody my age can't be trying to look for a new job in this economy."

Tanner nodded. "You're not going to get caught in the middle of anything. Bree is definitely a computer expert. If there's any chance Jared Ellis is manipulating his tracking monitor, she's going to find it."

"He's not," she said.

Tanner looked at her, lips in a thin line. "You're sure? You were able to check everything you needed to? They didn't stop you by showing up?"

She shrugged one shoulder. "They actually *helped* by showing up. I'm not an electronics expert, but I was able to figure out the workings of the anklet pretty easily. It's transmitting exactly the way it's supposed to. All backup systems and GPS tracking are online and calibrated correctly. It wasn't Jared who started the fire."

Tanner let out a low curse. "I don't know if that's better or worse."

"Trust me, I wanted it to be him. I tried damn near everything I could think of. If he's manipulating that monitoring system, he's smarter than me."

Tanner turned to her and tucked a strand of her

hair behind her ear. "Then he's not manipulating the system. Because he's definitely not smarter than you."

"If Jared isn't behind the fire, then who is?"

"That's what we've got to find out."

Chapter Eight

The image of Jared Ellis's hands on Bree was enough to send fire through Tanner's gut all the way back to Risk Peak. It had taken every ounce of control he possessed not to punch Ellis in the face, damn the consequences.

But that would've been a mistake that might have gotten the entire trial thrown out and made Jared a free man. Oscar Stobbart would've liked nothing better.

Bree was quiet on the way home. At first, he'd been worried that she'd been hurt and wasn't telling anyone, but she'd assured him that wasn't it, in a tight, almost distant voice. Bree wasn't a cranky or irritable person. If she was short with him, it was because that brilliant mind of hers was focusing intently on something else.

Most people could multitask, or at least hold a conversation with other people while thinking about something else. Not Bree. When she was focused on something, inconsequential things—like talking to people—got lost for her.

So while she was still trying to figure out how Jared might circumvent the monitoring system, Tanner knew better than to interrupt her thought process.

"I don't know how he could've done it," she finally whispered as they pulled up to the New Journeys building. "He might have paid someone else to start the fire, but I don't think there's any way he did it himself. I'm sorry."

Tanner reached over and cupped her cheek. "Don't be sorry. Eliminating a suspect is also helpful. It means we don't waste our time looking in that direction anymore."

"If he or anyone else tries to hack the ankle monitor, I've put stopgaps in place to notify me. Unless he's got someone smarter than me, there's no way he's going to get to Marilyn without us knowing."

He kissed her. "He doesn't have anyone smarter than you. I'm sure of it. So now we focus on finding who started the fire if it wasn't Jared."

He left her at New Journeys and spent the rest of the day attempting to do that and not getting very far. He and Ronnie were back to looking into the significant others of the residents of New Journeys and scouring over the fire inspector's report. Neither the timing mechanism nor the detonator matched any particulars of the fire department's list of known arsonists, so that was a dead end too.

Tanner's investigating brought him back around to Jared. Just because the man hadn't set the fire himself didn't mean he wasn't involved. The more Tanner looked into Jared's fraternity brothers, the less he liked what he saw. This was a tight-knit group. Even now, years after college, they still got together regularly. There seemed to be a group of five of them who were closest. Not all of them lived in Colorado, but most of them were here now, celebrating Jared's bail.

The preliminary background checks on all of them had come back clean. Tanner wasn't surprised. These guys were too smart to keep their dirty laundry out in the open.

But that didn't mean it wasn't there.

The trick was going to be catching them while keeping Marilyn safe.

Until Jared's trial, it looked like the protective shifts around Marilyn and her kids would need to continue. Tanner would do his part too, particularly because if danger was coming after Marilyn, it would definitely be too close to Bree for his liking.

He was ready to get married to her and have her right beside him every night. With their track record, he could pretty much guarantee trouble would still be coming, but at least he'd have her by his side where he could be sure to protect her.

Just twelve more days. Twelve more days and they'd be tied to each other forever.

He was smiling as he finally left the office at 8:00 p.m. and walked toward his car. Forever didn't scare him in the least.

"I don't even want to ask what that smile is all about." Noah was leaning against Tanner's SUV.

"Just happy to see you, brother, of course."

"Got time to hang out in Denver?"

Tanner rolled his eyes. "You know I've already been there once today, right?"

Noah pushed off from against the vehicle. "I know Bree said Ellis isn't hacking his ankle monitor—"

"He's not."

"—but I need eyes on him and his crew myself," Noah continued. "I'm going with or without you."

Tanner studied his brother. He didn't like the look in his eyes. "Then I'm going."

Noah gave him a surprised nod, like he had more arguments he could pull out if he needed to. He didn't need to. Tanner wasn't letting him go alone. After what happened this morning, things were already too delicate.

Tanner threw his bag into the back seat, then got in the driver's side. Noah got in on the passenger's side.

"I'm a little surprised you even told me you were going," Tanner said once they were a few miles down the road. Noah was more than capable of handling any sort of surveillance by himself.

He was capable of a hell of a lot more by himself too.

Noah shrugged. "I respect you, little brother. I respect that you chose the same route as Dad and choose to help uphold the law. And, even though I don't spend much time hanging out in the town itself, Risk Peak is my home."

"None of which actually explains why you invited me on this little adventure."

Noah stared straight out the windshield. "I needed someone I could trust."

"Trust to do what?"

"Trust to keep me from killing these bastards if the opportunity presents itself."

Those words coming from anyone else would've had Tanner shifting straight into law-enforcement mode. But this was his brother. So Tanner kept himself relaxed, even if he didn't really feel that way. "You know we have absolutely no proof that Jared or any of his cronies were involved with the fire."

Noah didn't say anything for a long time. "Ellis doesn't realize how lucky he is just to be still breathing after what he did to Marilyn."

Tanner's hands gripped the steering wheel more tightly. "Noah, you're going to have to let the system be his judge and jury. Not you." He glanced over at his brother. "Make no mistake, I will lock you up until after the trial to keep you from doing something stupid."

"It's why I've got you here," Noah muttered. He stared out the passenger window for a long time.

"I've seen stuff, Tanner. You know that. In special ops, I saw all sorts of violence against men, women and children that is the stuff nightmares are made of. But nothing I ever saw there puts me anywhere near the killing rage I feel when I think about Ellis hurting Marilyn."

Tanner wasn't sure his brother was aware of the reality of his own feelings. "You do know that's got more to do with Marilyn than it does Ellis, right?"

Noah's eyes, so much like Tanner's own, pinned him with a glare. "I know you're not trying to say what Ellis did was okay."

"Not at all. What I'm saying is that killing rage you feel isn't just because of his actions. It's because of him doing it to *her*." Tanner held a hand out to stop Noah's argument before it could go any further. "I'm not saying the bastard doesn't deserve to rot in jail. I'm just saying that rage you're talking about is because of her, not because of him."

Tanner returned his eyes to the road. Noah didn't say anything further as he processed it all. It may take Noah a while to recognize the truth, but he didn't lie to himself.

"I've been working with Marilyn," Noah finally said softly, still looking out the window. "Self-defense stuff, even before we knew Ellis's release was a possibility. She's so damn little. Doesn't seem to have any sort of warrior instinct. She's not like Bree, who survived on her own for so long. Marilyn is the type of woman who is meant to be cared for. She's not someone who should have to fight tooth and nail just to exist."

"Marilyn is stronger than you think. She has to be to have survived what she's survived."

Noah rubbed the top of his black hair—still cut military short even though he'd been out of the army for nearly five years now. "Oh, believe me, I know she's strong. I have never mistaken her quietness for weakness."

"You're doing the right thing, teaching her what

you can. Whatever she doesn't have as natural intu-
ition can be made up for with other skills. She may
not have the attack instinct…"

"But she can be taught other ways to make up
for that."

They were silent for long minutes.

"I want to fight her battles for her," Noah said.
"But I know that in the long run I'm doing a dis-
service to her by feeling that way. The best thing
I can do for her is teach her how to fight the mon-
sters herself."

Tanner waited for him to say more, but evidently,
he was done talking about it. It was the most he'd
heard his brother talk about anything personal in the
five years he'd been home.

Noah might be teaching Marilyn some things, but
it seemed she was teaching him some things, as well.

It wasn't long before they were pulling up at the
downtown Denver town house where Jared was staying. Neither of them said what both of them were
thinking: that something was definitely not right
when Ellis currently resided in a million-dollar home
while his wife and children lived in a shelter de-
signed for people without a home at all.

Tanner had researched this property earlier today.
"Town house is owned by a guy named Marius
Nixon. He's the same one who put the money up
for Jared's bail. Of all this little posse, Nixon is the
cleanest. I've got confirmation that he's not even in
the country right now."

Noah nodded, staring at the building. The window shades were open, allowing them to see inside to parts of the living room and dining room.

"The rest of Ellis's clan includes investment banker George Pearson, Paul Wyn, owner of a chain of restaurants, and of course his lawyer, Oscar Stobbart. None of them have ever been arrested or in any trouble with the law besides Ellis."

Noah grimaced. "Completely clean. Convenient."

"Almost squeakily so."

"Any of the rest of them married?"

"This is where it gets more interesting," Tanner said. "Both Pearson and Wyn had wives who died within the last five years."

"Isn't that an interesting coincidence?" Noah said. "No other wives around to ask if Jared's friends had been abusive also."

Tanner nodded. "Unfortunately, according to the coroner's reports, in both cases there was nothing suspicious about the deaths. One was a car accident. One was a skiing accident."

"If you had said cancer, I might have agreed it wasn't suspicious," Noah grunted. "But we both know a death that didn't get labeled as suspicious by the coroner's office could still be murder. But on paper they look like tragic characters who lost their loved ones and have never broken the law. Nice."

It was a tricky situation. Pearson and Wyn were both upstanding businessmen. They'd never done anything wrong in the eyes of the law. Accusing them of anything when their only questionable action was their association with Ellis—and he hadn't even been found guilty yet—would be career suicide for Tanner.

Tanner pulled out his laptop and ran the program Bree had created. "According to the ankle monitor, Jared is definitely inside the town house."

Noah pulled some binoculars out of his bag and trained them toward the building.

"Affirmative," he said after a few minutes. "I've spotted him inside. Pearson and Wyn are with him. Looks like they're having some sort of business meeting. Papers spread out all over the table. Maybe building plans or maps or something."

"I don't think any of them are in business with each other, but I haven't searched definitively. It's possible. None of them have business ties with Jared that we've found."

Noah put the binoculars back up to his eyes. "Well, whatever's happening here, Jared's definitely in charge. Now I wish I hadn't brought you."

"Why? You going to go in there and take them all out for looking over business plans?"

"No," Noah said. "If I wasn't with you, I'd already have surveillance equipment that would allow me to hear what they're talking about in there. No need to get a warrant."

Tanner let out a low curse, both because it would be so helpful to have that information, and also because it was so risky. "You have to be careful, Noah. Between me bringing in Bree to the bonding office today, and getting caught, if Ellis or Stobbart catch either of us nearby, it could affect the case. They might really have an argument for harassment."

"I'm not going to get caught. I don't want anything to jeopardize Ellis spending a good solid chunk of his life behind bars. But I'd still like to know what they're talking about and if it affects Marilyn."

"If it's maps and plans, it probably doesn't have anything to do with her. It's more likely business plans," Tanner said.

"Ellis seems pretty involved with those for someone who'll likely be going to prison soon."

They watched for another hour, passing the binoculars back and forth, as the men continued to discuss and argue over their plans inside the town house.

"Okay, they're on the move, putting on jackets." Noah put down his binoculars and both of them sank a little lower in their seats.

Jared and his friends came out the front door a few minutes later and entered an Uber that pulled up outside the door. Tanner handed Noah his tablet as he started the car.

"Make sure the updates about Jared's location coming to the computer are accurate and timely."

Staying far enough back not to be noticed, Tanner followed along behind the car.

"So far, pretty damn accurate," Noah muttered after a few minutes. "It's providing updates every thirty seconds and they seem to be very close to Jared's physical location."

Just further confirmation that the tracker was working.

They followed the car to a restaurant just within Jared's range, waited while they ate, then followed them to a strip club. Tanner barely refrained from rolling his eyes.

It really was like a group of overgrown frat boys getting together.

They stayed outside the strip club for another few hours until Ellis and his buddies stumbled out and back into another car to take them home.

Tanner didn't bother keeping as much distance from the vehicle this time. Ellis and his friends weren't doing anything suspicious, so they probably wouldn't be checking to see if they were followed, even if they were sober enough to do so.

"I guess this was a bust," Noah said as they parked across the street and watched Jared and company stumble back inside the town house. "I'm sorry I dragged you out half the night after you worked all day."

"You did the right thing. Better to have me with you if you're not sure you're going to be able to control yourself around Ellis. And at least we've got further confirmation that the tracker is calibrated correctly." Not that Tanner had much doubt after the work Bree had done.

Noah wiped a weary hand down his face as Tanner started the SUV. There wasn't any point in staying. "Do you really think Jared didn't have anything to do with the fire?"

"Him personally? No. I think the ankle monitor is solid. Hell, to be honest, I'm not even sure he paid someone to do it. And just because we don't like his buddies, it doesn't necessarily mean they're guilty of actual crimes, so we've got to be careful with this." Noah couldn't start throwing out accusations.

"I will be. After tonight I'm not even sure Jared had anything to do with it, eith- –" Noah's head jerked forward. "What the actual hell?"

Tanner spun his head to see what Noah was talking about and spotted Jared Ellis standing across the street, motioning with a finger for them to come closer.

Noah was out the car door and rushing toward Jared before Tanner knew what was happening. Noah was going to attack the man. Maybe not kill him, but definitely punch him.

It was exactly what Jared wanted.

"Noah!" Tanner ran—ignoring the honking horn and car that had to slam on its brakes to not hit him as he darted out in front of it. Noah was picking up speed and was almost to Jared.

Tanner ran, coming at his brother from the side in a flying tackle just before he reached out and landed a punch on Jared's jaw.

"Get off me, Tanner," Noah said through gritted teeth.

Tanner wrapped his arms around him in a bear hug. Strength for strength he and his brother were pretty evenly matched.

"It's what he wants, Noah." Tanner grunted as Noah's elbow caught him in the ribs. "Somebody's probably got a camera on us right now. You hit him and the whole case against him becomes shaky."

Jared was smiling at the both of them from just

a few feet away. There wasn't much Tanner would like more than to let Noah go so he could pound on the smug son of a bitch.

"The case is shaky anyway, Captain Dempsey. No matter what you or your brother do."

Noah stopped struggling. "How do you know who we are?"

Jared's cold smile got bigger. "I met Tanner earlier today when he had a non-law-enforcement employee impersonate a lab technician to harass me. But you, I understand, have been spending quite a bit of time with my wife."

"Soon to be ex-wife, you bastard," Noah spit out. He tapped Tanner on the arm. "I'm okay."

"You sure?"

"Yeah."

Tanner let his brother go, ready to tackle him again, if needed. But Noah had found his control, even if fury seemed to crackle off his body. Tanner got up and offered Noah a hand.

"You stay away from Marilyn and those kids." Noah's every word was clipped. "You want to get to them, you're going to have to go through me."

Jared tilted his head. "Marilyn will always be mine. All I need is a little time to persuade her of that."

Noah's eyes narrowed into slits. "Soon you'll be rotting away in prison, where you belong. You'll never be coming near Marilyn again."

"My lawyer had enough to get me out on bail.

Believe me when I say he has more than enough to keep me out of prison for good."

Now it was Tanner who took a step forward. "I don't think so, Ellis. I've seen the evidence. So enjoy your last few weeks of freedom. Or as much as you can in a two-mile radius. Because if you step one foot outside of that we're going to nail your ass."

Jared looked like he was going to charge Tanner, get violent, but stopped himself. Instead, he backed away slowly, holding his hands out in front of him. "I guess we'll see what happens at the trial. But if I was a betting man, I'd bet I walk out of the court a free man that day."

He winked at them and Tanner threw out an arm to catch Noah in case he lunged. But Noah had himself under control. Maybe more so than Tanner.

"And after the trial," Jared continued, backing up step-by-step. "I'll have as much time as I need to woo my wife back."

He turned and walked away. "See you at the trial, gentlemen," Jared called out over his shoulder. "I trust it won't be again before that."

Chapter Nine

They were able to move back into the New Journeys building three days later. The residents and townspeople worked together to get everything cleaned up and all their belongings transferred from the old building back to the new one.

Bree was still triple-checking Jared's ankle monitor every day, making sure her results matched what was being sent to the Denver marshals' office. She'd also spent at least a couple hours every day still trying to come up with a way Jared might try to outthink the system. She'd gone as far as to hack into the company itself to make sure everything was on the up-and-up.

It was.

Based on the conversation he and Noah had with the man, Tanner didn't think Jared was behind the fire. It was worse than that, if possible. Tanner was afraid Jared had something up his sleeve when it came to the trial. He told Bree about the brief conversation he and Noah had with Jared—how secure he'd felt that the trial was going to go his way.

Tanner had been poring over every piece of evidence he could find, determined to make sure there was nothing that had been missed that the prosecuting attorney might need.

And all of it weighed pretty heavily on Marilyn.

There hadn't been a peep from Jared or his ankle monitor. Bree had written a program so that if the monitor went off for any reason, it would send a notification to her computer and damn near everyone's phone. They wouldn't have to wait for anyone from Denver to notify them this time. They would know *instantly*.

But just the knowledge that Jared wasn't behind bars, that he was so confident about his upcoming trial, ate at Marilyn. She'd been barely keeping it together over the past few days since the fire.

Everyone was glad to be moving back into the new building with its heightened security and the general feeling of being back in their home. The fire would mean that the renovations scheduled for the next few months would have to be pushed back, but ultimately it wouldn't affect much now.

Cassandra was sitting in her office in the New Journeys building when Bree plopped down in a chair across from her after a day of carrying boxes up and down stairs.

"It's good to be home," Bree said.

"Yeah." Cassandra smiled, but it wasn't nearly as big as Bree would've thought.

"What's going on?"

"I'm going to have to cancel the camping trip. There's still too much going on with the insurance company and I just can't go. I can't be out of contact for three days right now, and there's zero cell phone coverage in that section of the wilderness."

Bree's heart sank. Eva and Sam had been looking forward to this trip so much. They would be devastated.

But maybe they didn't have to be.

"What about Tanner? He could lead the trip and do the teaching, right? I know he knows these woods well and as long as there's nothing going on in his office, he'd be willing to do it." She was sure of it. Nobody wanted to see these kids be disappointed.

Cassandra nodded. "Absolutely, he does. Dad used to take all three of us out all over these woods, and then they kept hunting and hiking even as they got older. That's not the issue."

"What is?"

"For insurance purposes, either you or I, as the directors of New Journeys, need to be there. Not to mention we can't send Tanner alone with three women, given their histories, no matter how upstanding of a guy he is."

Bree shrugged. "I'll go. A chance to watch my fiancé out in the wilderness he loves? I wouldn't mind witnessing that."

Cassandra tilted her head to the side and gave Bree a look that all but screamed that the other woman thought she was crazy. "You do know we're nine days from your wedding, right? What bride wants to go tromping off into the wilderness for three days a little more than a week before her wedding?"

"This bride right here." The more she thought about it, the more perfect the idea became. Nothing sounded better to Bree than getting away from all the wedding craziness. Maybe some relaxing in nature would help her brain come up with her vows, because she hadn't made one iota of progress on that.

And no amount of Jareds, ankle monitors or fires was going to stop the fact that she was getting married in nine days.

"I'll tell you what." Bree grinned at her future sister-in-law. "If you, Cheryl and Judy will handle all the wedding details for the next three days, I will talk Tanner into this camping trip slash rafting slash wilderness excursion. Believe me, I'm getting the better end of the deal."

Cassandra reached over her desk and they shook on it. "I'm already making most of the wedding decisions anyway, since you're hopeless at making decisions, so this will work out for both of us. The camping trip is officially back on."

When two little cheers and a round of giggles rang out in the hallway, Bree and Cassandra met each other's eyes and smiled.

The camping trip was back on.

THE BACKPACK ON Tanner's shoulders was a familiar and comfortable weight. Every step he took deeper into these woods made something inside him loosen and relax. How many times had Dad taken him, Noah and Cassandra out here over the years? Too many to count. Long after most teenagers weren't interested in hanging out with their parents anymore, he and Noah had still loved to come out here with their dad.

He loved the diversity of this area most of all. There were deep sections of forests and wilderness, then large patches of meadows that would open up out of nowhere, providing breathtaking views of the surrounding Rocky Mountains. There were thousands of square acres to lose yourself—or find yourself—in. And the Colorado River ran straight through it, at times gentle, but more often massive and majestic.

He'd been a little surprised when Bree called him up yesterday and asked him to lead the trip. He'd known how excited Eva and Sam were about it and would've agreed immediately as soon as he'd made sure there was nothing going on with the office.

But he was no dummy. When his bride-to-be started promising certain, *quite explicit*, sexual favors if Tanner would make time to do this, he'd pretended like his calendar was much fuller than it actually was. And he intended to collect on every last sweet, sexy and surprisingly dirty thing she'd offered to trade on their wedding night.

Although the temptation to go pick her up right then and get started had been very difficult to resist.

But looking at the faces surrounding him now, he was doubly glad he'd been able to take the time to lead this little expedition.

Sam and Eva, both carrying appropriately sized backpacks, were beaming from ear to ear. The two other children who were supposed to have come on the trip had to cancel, but that had not dampened the kids' spirits. Marilyn didn't beam, but at least for once she didn't look like the weight of the world was crashing down on her shoulders as she walked forward carrying a backpack not much bigger than Sam's. Tanner had made sure that was the case. The woman just needed to relax and enjoy herself rather than worry about the heavy lifting. She had done the heavy lifting for long enough.

The other two women, Barb and Francis, he didn't know very well, but they seemed to be enjoying themselves as they chatted quietly and walked.

Maybe most surprising was who brought up the rear of their group: Noah. His brother had shown up this morning at the place where they'd be leaving the cars, backpack ready.

If Tanner thought Sam had been happy before, the sight of his hero showing up to go on the camping trip nearly put him over the moon. The little boy hadn't been more than ten feet from Noah all day.

Tanner didn't press his brother for details about why he was here. He'd spent more time in Risk Peak in the last five days than he had since he'd gotten out of the army. Noah trusted Bree's research on the ankle monitor but wanted to be nearby Marilyn just in case.

Tanner didn't care why his brother was here. It was good to have a second person he could count on 100 percent in wilderness situations.

He knew he could count on Bree also. His computer genius had become quite the outdoors woman over the past few months. But this wilderness—as beautiful as it was—could turn deadly in a dozen ways before you could even blink.

"Everything good?" Bree's hand slid into his and she smiled up at him.

"Perfect. We're right on track and right on schedule. Not that we have anything too aggressive planned, since our group is made up of quite a few novices."

"Excited novices."

He smiled and took a sip of water out of his canteen before offering it to her. "Those are the best kind." He leaned closer so only she could hear him. "You know I would've done this without all those special...*favors* you offered."

She smiled as she sipped the water. "That's okay. I didn't even get to the really good stuff I was going to offer if I thought you wouldn't say yes."

Tanner couldn't keep in his bark of laughter. This woman. He'd created a monster when he'd taken her to bed nearly a year ago. The very best, most sexy kind of monster. And he got to keep her as his own personal monster for the rest of his life.

"I can't wait to get married to you," he whispered, reaching closer to nuzzle behind her ear with his nose.

"I'm just glad to leave all the wedding planning to your sister and the other gals. This will allow them to do what they've wanted to do for a while—get rid of the feet-dragging, decision-phobic bride. They'll be able to get stuff done a lot quicker without me there.

Plus, they can't force me to try on my wedding dress again if I'm off hiking with you."

"Are you sure you're okay being gone this close to the wedding?"

She grabbed his shirt and pulled him close, rising up on her tiptoes to give him a kiss. "More than sure. Believe me, there's nowhere else I'd rather be."

They turned to look at Noah, who was crouched down, showing Sam and Eva something in the wildlife behind them.

"You didn't tell me Noah was coming," Bree said. "I was surprised."

"I didn't know he was coming. I haven't talked to him since we paid Jared our little visit. I know Noah's been around, keeping tabs on Marilyn and the kids as often as possible."

"Anything new regarding Jared?"

He rubbed his eyes with his thumb and fingers. "No. I'm still poring over the files. Still trying to find anything that might prove he was connected to the fire. Ronnie and I even went out and questioned Paul Wyn and George Pearson, to see if they had alibis for the night of the fire."

"And let me guess, they did."

"Yes. Each other, and Jared."

She let out a sigh. "Convenient. I just feel so frustrated that I can't do more."

He wrapped an arm around her shoulder as Noah began leading the group forward again. "How about no thinking about Jared today. No thinking about the case or the ankle monitor. No tulle. Only thinking about the majestic beauty surrounding us and making this trip as memorable for the kids as possible."

She leaned into his side. "You had me at the words *no tulle*."

Chapter Ten

The tents were set up and everyone was settled in for the night when Tanner came out to sit next to Noah at the fire.

They made it to the camping site with no problem and had caught fish in the stream tributary of the Colorado River they'd be coasting on tomorrow. By the time they'd finished making the s'mores with the ingredients Tanner had sneaked in as a special surprise, the smile on everyone's face had been near giddy.

Except Noah's.

Not that his brother was ever going to be much of a talker or smiler, but he was definitely tenser now than he had been when they first started the hike.

"What's going on?" Tanner asked softly. He didn't want anyone else to hear this conversation.

"Nothing I can put my finger on."

Tanner sat down on the log across from his brother. "But you're thinking there might be trouble?"

"I don't have concrete evidence of anything."

Noah looked around into what anyone else would consider to be peaceful darkness.

Tanner rolled his eyes. "I'll take your gut feeling over 99 percent of the population's concrete evidence any day."

Noah was quiet for a long minute. "I'm not sure I can trust my gut too much either, to be honest. But there's nobody around us right now, that much I know for sure. I set up a few observation traps that would let me know if anybody had been surveilling us. When I checked them a few minutes ago there was no evidence of anybody else around."

"Could be stress wearing on you. That talk with Jared definitely didn't put me at ease."

"That's for damn sure. Bastard was way too confident he wouldn't be convicted at the trial. Like he knows something we don't."

Tanner nodded, lips tight. Oscar Stobbart already put a call in to Sheriff Duggan, Tanner's boss. Nothing formal, just a verbal complaint and concern about harassment against his client. Fortunately, they didn't have an ID for Bree, so there was nothing official Oscar could do. But Tanner had no doubt this would come up again at the trial if Stobbart could possibly work it in.

"Have you been following Jared more? We don't want to do anything that gives Stobbart any reason to try to have the case dismissed outright."

"I've got a colleague who's gone into Denver a couple of times for me, with instructions to stay far from Jared. I do know they've still got those building plans and maps out everywhere. Stobbart has joined them most nights. Another man joined them last night."

"That's probably Marius Nixon, the guy who provided money for Jared's bail. He arrived back in the country yesterday."

Noah rolled his shoulders. "They're planning something, Tanner."

"Do you know that for sure? Has your guy been using the surveillance equipment you talked about?" Anything the man heard wouldn't be allowable in court, but at this point, Tanner would be glad just to have information. Once they knew what was going on, they'd figure out a plan later.

"I know there's something going on because my man couldn't hear anything with his surveillance equipment. They're using counter surveillance equipment."

Tanner let out a low curse.

Noah nodded. "That's how I felt too. It's high-end stuff. Took my man a night to figure out the info he was receiving wasn't legit. He happened to hear a loop in the recording their equipment was spitting out. Most people wouldn't have caught it at all."

"What do you think they're planning?" Tanner leaned closer to the fire, trying to process all of this.

"Honestly, I think they have something up their sleeves for the trial, then are planning to take Marilyn and the kids somewhere. I'm not going to let that happen, Tanner."

Tanner nodded. "*We're* not going to let that happen. Not you, not me, not Bree, not anyone else at

New Journeys or in Risk Peak. Marilyn and those kids are one of ours now. You're not alone in this. Neither is she."

Noah shrugged. "It's hard for me not to work alone."

"We've got almost four months until the trial. We know the ankle monitor is working, so we focus on figuring out their plan. In this case, the best offense is a good defense. But we've got to let the law handle this. We cannot go after them just because they're doing suspicious stuff."

"Roger that."

"So let's try to enjoy this camping trip and make it something memorable for Marilyn and the kids. Unless you think there's actual danger here."

Noah ran a hand through his thick black hair that looked so much like Tanner's own. "Honestly, I don't know. I feel like something is off, but my neutrality is definitely compromised when it comes to that woman and those kids. Maybe I want Jared to be here so that I have an excuse to take him out and make sure they're safe for the rest of their lives."

"As an officer of the law, I'm afraid I'd probably have to let you do exactly that if Jared showed up here." Tanner gave his brother a wide grin.

"I have the emergency radio," Tanner said after a few minutes. "If there's any change in Jared's status, Ronnie will let us know right away."

"Good. There's probably nothing out there right

now except my own feelings of inadequacy haunting me."

"Well, you better let those die out in the cold, because we're going to need your help protecting Marilyn if Jared really is found innocent by some miracle. And I need you on this trip because those kids certainly look up to you. Especially Sam."

Noah shrugged. "That's good, because I look up to them too. And especially their mom."

That was about as gushing and flowery as Noah got. Tanner swallowed his chuckle, but not quickly enough.

"Stuff it, jackass," Noah muttered.

"Yes, sir. How about I take first shift on lookout, just in case? We've got a long day of hiking and rafting ahead of us tomorrow."

None of it would be very rough—nobody wanted to take young children on rapids they couldn't handle—but it would be a full and exciting day.

"Wake me up in a couple hours and I'll relieve you."

Tanner settled into his place by the fire, listening for changes in the night noises around him. That would be his first indication that danger was nearby. He looked up at the moon, barely visible through the trees. Standing guard was no hardship for him. Maybe Noah was right, and his gut feelings were just a manifestation of the frustration inside him for not being able to do anything about the abuse Marilyn had suffered.

But either way, Tanner would be ready in case danger came.

BEING OUT HERE in the woods was so much better than wedding planning, but it didn't take Bree long to recognize tension in both Noah and Tanner the next day.

It wasn't overt—they were both still teaching and smiling, at least as much as Noah ever smiled, and they seemed to be having a good time. But there was a tension in Tanner—an awareness—that hadn't been there yesterday when they'd started their trip.

"What's going on?" she asked when they stopped for water. She'd been watching him all morning and all through their lunch break. Watching him watch the area around them, looking for threats.

"Nothing's going on. Why do you ask?"

She narrowed her eyes at him. "I don't know. Maybe because I've seen you around enough dangerous situations to recognize the I'm-about-to-turn-into-supercop look? What aren't you telling me?"

He pulled her against him and kissed her temple. "Nothing. I promise. Nothing concrete. Noah just got a little spooked—although it ended up being nothing—and both of us just want to be diligent."

"But nothing happened besides Noah's Spidey senses tingling?"

He smiled and kissed her. "Nothing. I promise I'll tell you if I think you need to be concerned."

"Really? You have been known to keep things from me before. Important things—because you wanted to handle it all by yourself."

"Believe me, I've learned my lesson when it comes to keeping things from you. We are a team."

Bree kissed him and turned back to the group.

She watched as Noah took a sip of his water, wiping his mouth with the back of his hand afterward. Sam, sitting right beside him, mimicked the motion almost exactly a couple seconds later.

They spent the next two hours making steady progress through the wilderness. Tanner and Noah took multiple opportunities to indicate different plants and animals along the way. They showed some edible berries, but then were quick to point out the poisonous berries that looked very similar.

They identified poison oak and other plants to avoid, as well as specifying the multiple different trees and flowers that made up the beauty of this part of Colorado. Their respect for the wilderness around them was evident in every sentence. It was nearly impossible not to get caught up in their passion for the land.

The running theme was obvious: *respect nature*. Nature wasn't always gentle, but even in its harshness there was beauty.

They came across all sorts of animals. The racer snake they saw along one rocky ridge was Sam's personal favorite, even though it had everybody else squealing in fear.

Noah pointed out the tracks from deer and elk, and even the signs that a bear had passed through at some point. When Eva's eyes grew wide, Tanner took the time to explain the best way to defend yourself against a bear was actually to avoid it in the first place. Talking out loud and letting a bear know you were nearby was the best way to get it to move along in the opposite direction. Most bears weren't looking for a confrontation.

Sam wanted to press about what should be done if the bear didn't move along and charged instead, but that topic of conversation was obviously a little upsetting for Eva, who was soon near tears. A look and nod passed between Tanner and Noah, before Tanner grabbed Eva's hand to show her a caterpillar that was climbing up a tree. Noah placed a light hand on Sam's shoulder and led him a few steps over to the side.

Concern clouded Marilyn's face.

"Don't worry," Bree whispered to her. "Noah won't let the details get too out of hand. Although the way Sam got excited about that snake, I think he could probably handle details about a bear attack."

"Oh." Marilyn relaxed. "A bear attack. Right. Yeah, Sam can handle that."

Marilyn hadn't been worried about the topic, Bree realized.

"You know Noah would never hurt Sam, right?" she whispered.

Marilyn gave a shaky laugh. "I know that. Of course, I know that."

"Oh, my gosh, really? That's awesome!" Sam's excited voice called out from next to Noah, who was obviously imparting some vast wilderness secret to the boy. "It's so gross! Mom would never do it." Sam belly-laughed.

They watched as Noah leaned his head closer to tell Sam something else.

"I don't want him to live his life scared," Marilyn whispered. "I already hate myself enough for what I let them witness happen to me. I don't want to spend their whole childhood hovering over them and making them afraid to try new things and befriend new people."

Bree ran a hand along her friend's back, the gesture coming so much more naturally now than it would have a year ago, since she now had so many people in her life teaching her how to give and receive love.

"The world isn't always a safe place. Your kids learned that early, and, yeah, that's a tragedy of gargantuan proportions. But look at them, Marilyn." She gestured first at Eva, who was holding Tanner's hand and pressing her face close to a tree so she could see the critter, giggling every few seconds. Then over to Sam, who was staring at Noah with huge, wide eyes, obviously completely entranced with whatever the man was saying.

"Yeah?" Marilyn asked. "They don't seem to be doing anything particularly amazing."

Bree smiled. "Exactly. They're kids getting excited about caterpillars and probably some gross story about peeing on a tree to keep away a bear. And they're fine. Whatever you did, whatever you suffered through to protect them? It worked."

"I'm totally going to try that!" Sam yelled.

Noah chuckled. It was the first time Bree had heard him laugh. Even Tanner turned around at the sound.

"We'll check with your mom first. And you definitely have to make sure there is an adult around."

Noah looked over and winked at Marilyn, causing her to blush. Bree bit her tongue to keep from teasing her about it.

"Noah and I have been spending a little bit of time together," Marilyn said so softly Bree could hardly hear her.

"Spending time together as in dating?"

Marilyn flushed even more. "Not really. I mean he did have dinner with us once last week before the fire."

Bree nudged her hip against her friend. "That sounds a little bit like a date."

"Mostly he comes by after the kids go to bed at night."

Bree tried not to do a double take at that news. Certainly, they were both consenting adults, and although Marilyn may be technically still married to Jared on paper, it was safe to say the marriage had ended sometime around when he'd dislocated her shoulder, broken her nose, cracked her ribs, fractured her wrist and sent her into a coma.

If Marilyn could find a little bit of happiness with Noah—and vice versa—then damn all the people who would judge her for it. But Bree was still a little surprised.

"Good for you. I say get as much action as you can."

Marilyn's jaw dropped and her eyes got wide. "Oh, my God, it's not like that. Noah doesn't come over to have sex." Although the woman didn't look too distraught about that idea. "He's been teaching me self-defense moves."

Now, *that* sounded like Noah.

"Well, there's no one better you could learn them from," Bree said, meaning it.

"I know."

"And heck, that sort of is dating for Noah."

"I know," Marilyn whispered again.

Tanner and Noah got everyone moving forward again, focusing more on the smaller, gentler animals rather than predators. They answered any questions the kids or Barb or Francis had, while Bree and Marilyn brought up the rear.

They'd gone about another thirty minutes when Tanner stopped and pointed out a group of marmots lying out on a rock, far enough from the humans not to be threatened. Noah handed everyone his binoculars so they could take a closer look at the large ground squirrels.

"Marmots are pretty cool," Tanner said. "They eat grass and flowers and live in groups of between ten and twenty. During warm weather, they pretty much spend all day eating and lying out in the sun, getting fat."

"Sounds kind of boring," Sam said.

Tanner rubbed the kid's hair. "The amazing thing about marmots is that they hibernate over half their lives. At least six months out of every year, they're underground, living inside a hole, just trying to survive."

"They stay inside a hole for six months?" Eva asked. "They don't come out to eat or anything?"

Tanner tapped her on her nose. "Nope. They just hunker down, breathe in and out, and survive. That's it."

"Boring," Sam muttered again.

"I have no idea how Tanner knows all this stuff," Bree murmured to Marilyn. "I'm not sure if it's the nerdiest thing I've ever seen or the sexiest."

She glanced over at Marilyn, but she was just staring out blankly ahead of her.

"You okay?" Bree asked.

"I'm a marmot," Marilyn finally said. "Spending half my life living in a hole, just trying to survive. That's basically what I've done."

She said it so softly there was no way anyone else could've possibly heard her.

But when Noah spoke again, he was looking directly at her. "I don't think marmots are boring at all. I think they're pretty amazing. They don't really have any true defense mechanisms like other animals do, and it's just sheer strength of will that keeps them alive during the winter. They survive because they are determined to. That's something to be respected."

Marilyn finally looked away from Noah.

"All right," Tanner said. "Let's get going. We've got about another mile until we get to the rafts."

Everyone picked up their pace. The rafting was the highlight of the trip for Sam. He liked the tents and the wilderness and whatever crazy stuff Noah had told him about escaping bears, but rafting was truly exciting.

"We'll only be on the water a couple hours," Tanner said. "And there aren't any real rapids until much farther down the river."

Sam let out a disappointed groan. Tanner chuckled and ruffled his hair. "How about you get some rafting experience under your belt today and we'll start building up from there. Everybody has to learn in the safe water."

"I'll bet you and Noah didn't have to learn in baby water like this," Sam said when they reached the area where the rafts were stored.

"Not only did we learn in water just like this, we learned in this *exact* water," Noah said. "Lips wasn't much more than your age, and I was just a couple years older when our dad brought us here for the first time. So don't be talking junk about this water."

Sam's eyes grew big. "Really? You first went rafting *here*?"

"Yep," Tanner said. "And a year later I was already doing class III rapids. So let's get to work."

Sam was a lot more focused after finding out this was where his two idols got their start.

Like they'd done everything else, Tanner and Noah carefully explained the logistics of rafting. Noah readily admitted that Tanner was the better raftsman, although Bree was sure he could do it just fine.

Tanner pulled the map out of his backpack and showed everyone exactly where they'd be going.

"At this second fork, we'll take the left. Farther downriver is where the rapids get a little more exciting than what we're looking for today." He winked at Sam. "But maybe soon. If it's okay, Bree Cheese and I and the two rug rats will go down with the majority of the supplies. Noah will have the honor of escorting the rest of the lovely ladies."

Bree was going to offer to trade with Marilyn so she could be with her kids. But when she heard the other woman mutter "no marmot," she held her tongue. Marilyn was trying to face her fears by allowing the kids to be away from her. Bree wanted to help.

And when Noah gave Marilyn a reassuring nod and a small smile, Bree was even more convinced this was the right thing.

Soon they were on their way. The first hour on the river Bree just sat back and enjoyed herself. The water was moving at a fast enough pace to keep everybody interested and it felt like nothing could go wrong out here. The kids kept demanding Noah and Tanner race, and they took turns paddling hard to get in front of each other. About thirty minutes later they came up on the second fork and Tanner let Noah pull ahead.

"Aw, man," Sam said. "They're beating us!"

Tanner just smiled. "Noah's got to get ahead so he can help us dock and get the supplies out. And come on, you and I both know we could take them."

"Yeah, we could!"

Tanner slowed them down further with his oar as

Noah took the fork. Bree could see why he wanted to have Noah already stopped and ready to help them. The speed of the water had definitely picked up.

She was just about to ask him about it when an odd screeching noise came from the front of the raft. She looked back at Tanner, who was steering them with the paddle. "Do you hear that?"

When the sound got louder a moment later, everyone could hear it.

Tanner's muttered curse was cut off when the raft jerked suddenly, the front end collapsing, throwing them all forward.

Both kids screamed as they were thrown forcefully into the water. Bree grabbed for Eva, but the rapids pulled her away, then pulled Bree under.

Chapter Eleven

Tanner didn't even waste time trying to figure out what the hell had caused a large enough puncture in the PVC material of the raft to cause it to collapse so suddenly. They weren't near any severely jagged rocks, and even if they were, the raft material should've been able to handle it.

Instead he pushed off the remainder of the raft that was still above water and dived forward into the water.

The cold of it stunned him for second. It might have been May, but the water flowing down from the Rockies was still damn cold. And Bree and the kids were in it with not nearly the muscle mass he had to fight the cold.

All of them were wearing life jackets, but someone could still drown in one if they fought it or got pulled under the wrong way.

Out of the corner of his eye the fork where they needed to have turned floated by. There was no way they could make it over in this current, and now there was no way Noah would be able to get here to help them out. It was all up to him now.

Bree's voice reached him over the roar of the water. "Tanner... I... Sam... Find Eva!"

Praying that meant Bree had Sam, Tanner propelled himself as high up in the water as he could in his sopping clothes and boots to try to see. Two bright life jackets were closer to the shore. The other one, smaller—it had to be Eva—was still flailing in the middle of the rushing water. Tanner began to swim toward her with every bit of strength he had. If Eva got washed too far down the river, she'd be in the serious rapids.

He pushed himself hard, shoving away the fear that even though Bree and Sam were closer to the shore, they could still be in danger. Bree had become quite the outdoors woman, but this could be more than she could handle.

Saying a silent prayer on his bride-to-be's behalf, he swam the last dozen yards between him and Eva.

"Eva, I'm coming sweetheart!"

"L-Lips? I'm cold."

Her scared voice tugged at his heart, but she was alive. That was the most important thing.

"I'm coming up behind you and then we're gonna swim together to the shore."

"I'm not a good swimmer."

"You're doing just fine. Doing perfect, considering none of us had planned to be swimming down this river today, did we?" He closed the last yard, his fingertips grabbing the back of her life vest. "Got you."

"I—I didn't know what to do. I'm cold."

He pulled her up against his chest, wrapping his arm under her armpits, and began swimming toward the shore. "You did perfect. Absolutely perfect."

"Where's Sam?"

"He's with Bree. They are probably already on the shore. Let's go find them." Tanner prayed that was true.

Eva really was a little trouper. She didn't panic, didn't cry, just used her little legs as best she could to help propel them toward the shore. He'd known grown-ass adults who hadn't kept as much composure as this five-year-old girl did in the face of danger.

They made it to shore a few exhausting minutes later. Tanner made sure Eva was all the way out and safe before standing to see if he needed to go back into the water for Bree and Sam. His heart began thumping harder in his chest when he didn't see any sign of either life vest on the shore or in the water.

"Bree!" His voice came out much weaker than he wanted it to.

He wasn't even sure what direction he should look. He hadn't seen either of them after catching them out of the corner of his eye when he first went after Eva. Maybe they hadn't made it to the shoreline. Maybe they had gotten sucked back into the water and were rushing downstream.

"Bree!" he called again. When he didn't get an answer, he ran toward a boulder that would give him a better vantage point of the riverbank and the water itself. He scrambled up the rock, cursing as he fell, movements uncoordinated from the cold, scraping his hands. He ignored it. There would be time for first aid later.

From this higher vantage point he spotted Bree and Sam immediately. A relieved breath shuddered out of his chest when he saw they were alive and conscious. They were both hovering over one of the side whirlpools the rapids made, reaching for something.

Tanner scrambled back down the rock to get Eva, and they made their way over to Bree and Sam, Tanner carrying Eva's shivering body most of the way.

"Oh, thank God," Bree said when she saw them. She then tried to stand, clutching the emergency bag that they'd obviously fished out of the whirlpool to her chest.

"This bag has rope," she said between chattering teeth.

"Smart," he said, pulling her to his chest and letting Eva slide to the ground. If Bree had needed to get him out of the water, that rope would've been the best way to do it. Possibly the only way to do it.

"That bag has emergency supplies—Mylar blankets and waterproof matches. If we could only save one backpack, that's the one we want." He turned to the kids. "We're going to build a fire and we're going to get warm. I know this sounds weird, but I need everybody to strip down to just your T-shirts and undies."

He knew they were cold when nobody gave him any complaints. Tanner and Sam began gathering firewood while Bree helped the shivering Eva off with her wet clothes.

"I can get this, buddy, if you want to go get your wet clothes off. I know you're cold."

"I'll—I'll help," Sam said through chattering teeth. "The sooner we get wood, the sooner we'll have a fire."

They began picking up twigs and branches. At least it hadn't rained, so nothing was wet.

Tanner nodded at the boy. "That's exactly what my father said to Noah and me when we fell into this river when we weren't much older than you."

"Really?"

"Yep. And I know your mom would be so proud of how brave and strong you're being. Noah too. Don't tell him I told you, but when he fell in the river, he cried like a little baby."

Arms full of wood, they headed back toward Bree and Eva.

"Noah really cried?" Sam asked.

"Yeah, of course, and I was crying too. It was damn cold." That got a small laugh from Sam.

Bree was holding a sleeping Eva on her lap wrapped in a blanket when they got to them.

Tanner began building a fire. Normally he would have taken this opportunity to teach Sam about it, but Sam probably wasn't up to learning much right now, and getting the fire going quickly was of the essence.

"She okay?" he asked Bree.

Bree rocked the girl back and forth in her arms. "Once I got her warm and fed her a protein bar, she was out like a light."

"Did you get something to eat too?"

"Yes. There isn't a lot in that bag, but I'm thankful for a little bit of food."

Tanner got the blaze going, then reached down and pulled off his wet jeans, glad he had boxers on. He held out the other thermal blanket to Sam, who took it, then removed his own wet clothing.

"I feel like I could sleep for a week. Getting tossed around like that takes it out of you."

"What happened?" Bree asked. "Did we run into a rock or something?"

Tanner looked over at Sam. The kid's eyes were already drifting shut. He grabbed a protein bar from the bag, unwrapped it and put a bite in the boy's mouth. He chewed without protest. Tanner took a bite himself, then put the rest of it in Sam's mouth.

"It shouldn't have mattered if we'd run into a rock. Rafts like that are meant to hit rocks regularly."

Feeling much better without his wet clothes on, Tanner grew the fire until it was a large blaze. Sam was already falling asleep on the ground next to him.

"The bag you saved wasn't the one with the emergency sat phone, was it?"

Bree shook her head. "No, it wasn't your backpack. It was the emergency kit Barb was carrying. Blankets, some food, a water bladder and a flare gun."

"Flare gun. That's good."

"Do we need it?" she asked.

"Only to signal to the others that we made it and we're okay. I'm sure Marilyn is beside herself right now."

Bree pulled Eva more closely into her arms. "I would be too if I saw my kids go headfirst into a river and there was nothing I could do about it."

He got up and walked over to the wet backpack. Pulling out the flare gun, he also grabbed two of the four flares in the package.

"Two flares will let Noah know we don't need any assistance. Otherwise he'll be trying to sprint his way to us. Getting to the nearest bridge would take him hours, even at full speed. We don't want him doing that—the risk of injury is too high in the dark if we don't need help."

He kissed Bree on top of the head as he walked by to get far enough away not to wake the kids as he shot. He pulled out the flare gun, loaded and shot it, then repeated the process. He knew Noah would understand the message and just hoped he'd be able to keep Marilyn calm.

He added more firewood to the fire, then resumed his seat next to Sam.

"So what's the plan?" Bree asked, attempting to smother a huge yawn. "We've got, what, an hour or two before sunset?"

"Plan really doesn't change too much from the original camping plan, except to cut it short." Tanner looked up at the trees that were starting to sway more. "Honestly, we probably would've needed to cut the trip short anyway. The wind is picking up, which is going to blow in the storm that was coming this way a little faster."

She made a face. "Are we going to get rained on? I'm just getting dry."

"No, not tonight. Maybe late tomorrow night. But we'll be able to make it back to the vehicles by then. We'll meet Marilyn, Noah and the others at the first bridge where they can cross. Noah will know to rendezvous with us there. Besides that, we'll still have fun, learn as much about nature and the wilderness as possible and the kids will have a hell of a story to tell as they grow up about the time they almost drowned in the Colorado River."

She smiled. "I like that plan."

"We've got plenty of water and a way to carry it, some edible plants around and the basic supplies to fish tonight and tomorrow. We'll have to cut the trip short, but all in all, nothing too bad."

Bree shifted, scooting over so she could lean more of her weight back against a large rock behind her. She moved the sleeping Eva over so she was on the ground, but still next to her.

"Have you ever had anything like this happen before? I know you rafted in this area your whole life. What would've happened if something like that occurred once we'd hit the bigger rapids?"

He stretched his legs out in front of him, finally feeling, if not quite warm, at least not freezing. "No, I've never had anything like this happen to me, or even heard anything like it. And these rafts were inspected before they were brought here. A puncture would've been noticed."

"It definitely wasn't a slow leak. We jerked like we hit something."

"That shouldn't have made a difference either. These rafts are qualified for up to class V rapids. If they burst every time you hit a rock, there'd be people floating down the river all over the place."

And that was the problem, wasn't it? The raft had *burst*. Even if there had been some odd puncture, it should have been a slow leak, not that sort of explosion.

"I wish I could get my hands on the raft," he continued. "It had to have been some sort of manufacturer malfunction. It was dangerous enough as is, but like you said, on bigger rapids it could have been deadly."

"Could someone have tampered with the raft?"

Tanner thought about that for a minute. About the danger Noah had been sensing. But it just didn't make sense. "The short answer is yes."

Bree sighed, shifting her weight. "But the longer answer is that it wouldn't really make sense to tamper with the raft."

"Exactly. Too many unknown variables. We didn't decide who was going to be in each raft until just a couple minutes before we got in them. Plus, we were never in very dangerous waters. If we had been in the other raft, and Noah, Marilyn, Barb and Francis had been in ours, they would've just immediately swum to shore. Nothing but a big headache."

Bree wrapped her arms around her knees. "I guess I'm just jumpy after the fire and all the Jared stuff."

Yeah, Tanner didn't like that he now did not have any sort of communication with Risk Peak. Ronnie couldn't send him an update if something happened with Jared. And his Glock was now sitting at the bottom of the Colorado River. It was time to get home.

Tanner got up and moved over until he was sitting next to her, on the opposite side of the sleeping Eva, and wrapped an arm around her shoulders. "It's been a crazy couple of weeks, that's for sure. And in camping my dad always said you could count on some sort of calamity, but I'll be honest, I wasn't expecting this."

"Well, hopefully we've gotten our share of bad luck all used up. None left for the wedding."

He kissed her temple. "Nothing with us ever seems to go according to plan, does it?"

She snuggled into him. "Do you think that will be true our whole life?"

"Let's hope not. I hereby decree that we have officially gotten all our bad luck out of our system. From here on out, no more calamities."

"I'll second that."

They stared into the fire until they were both nice and warm. Tanner put his hiking pants and boots back on as the sun started to set. Sam woke up and the two of them headed to the river for fishing. Tanner explained about the flares so that the boy would know his mother wouldn't be worried.

They ate enough to at least not be hungry, then

gathered firewood to have nearby to keep the blaze going all night.

They used what they could from the rescued emergency pack for pillows and covering. It was going to be a long night, but all things considered, it could've been much, much worse.

Chapter Twelve

Both kids were chattering nonstop the next morning as the four of them made their way toward the rendezvous point. They weren't in any hurry; coming from this side of the river meant they had a much shorter walk than Noah and the women did.

They'd eaten an odd breakfast of fish and protein bars, but it had given them the nourishment they needed.

Eva and Sam were bantering back and forth, talking at great length about all the details they were going to tell their friends—falling into the water, the snake, Sam's intel about how to avoid a bear.

Tanner met Bree's eyes, both of them struggling not to smile, as the kids decided that they would leave out any really scary parts so that their friends wouldn't be so frightened of rafting that they were afraid to try it.

"Wise." Bree nodded her head as she walked hand in hand with Eva. "You don't want to overwhelm your friends with too much action all at once."

They'd gone another mile before Sam lengthened

his stride so he could be walking next to Tanner, leaving the females a little farther behind. The kid obviously had something to say.

"What's on your mind, buddy?"

"Do you think Noah is going to be mad at us?"

"Why would he be mad?"

Sam shrugged. "Because we had all the food and supplies in our boat. And he didn't really have anyone to help them out. Just Mom and Miss Barb and Miss Francis."

Tanner swallowed a laugh. "Although I'm sure he would have rather had you there to help him, Noah is capable of handling just about anything. Even three women who don't know much about the wilderness. Although your mom is pretty darn smart."

Sam nodded solemnly. "Oh, I know. But she's…"

Tanner knew the kids had been seeing a child psychologist. He wished he had a doctor's advice on what to say right now to the little boy. He would just go with his gut.

"She's what, buddy?"

"Broken," he whispered, then touched his chest. "On the inside. My dad…he hurt her."

"A man should never hurt a woman."

"I know." Sam's voice got smaller. "I tried to help, but Dad would lock us in our bedrooms."

"Hey." Tanner stopped and crouched down beside him so they could be eye to eye. The girls came up on them, but Bree just kept walking, giving them privacy.

"I know you and I don't know each other very

well." He smiled and winked at the boy. "Although after our river adventure, I think we have a bond, right?"

Sam nodded solemnly. "Yes, sir."

"Then I want to say this man to man. Friend to friend. That stuff your dad did to your mom is on *him*, and nobody else. Not her, and especially not you or Eva. A real man should never raise a hand against a woman. Even if you could've gotten out of that room you were locked in, there's nothing you could've done."

Sam didn't look like he believed Tanner, but Tanner hadn't expected him to. It was going to take more than just a couple of sentences from someone the kid didn't really know very well to unpack all the emotional damage done in this situation. All any of them could do was to continuously reassure Sam, and Marilyn, that they weren't at fault for Jared Ellis's actions.

"Hey, you're not worried that Noah will hurt your mom, are you? Because I can assure you that will never happen."

"I know Noah wouldn't hurt her. I just didn't want him to get mad at her because she sometimes has bad days. Sometimes it's hard for her to get out of bed. Sometimes she cries."

God, Tanner's heart was breaking for this kid. When he and Noah had been this age, their biggest concern had been trying to talk their mom into letting them stay out past when the streetlights came on, and how to do enough car washes and lemonade stands to raise the money to buy the video game they currently wanted. There had been all sorts of laughter and chaos in their house. Never violence, and rarely tears.

"Don't you worry about Noah." Tanner stood and squeezed Sam's shoulder, and they began walking again. "You know Miss Cassandra is our sister, right? And she's kinda crazy. So Noah can definitely handle your mom, even if she's not having a good day."

"Oh, yeah." A smile broke through on Sam's solemn face. "Miss Cass is a little crazy. She's not quiet like Bree Cheese or my mom."

Tanner rolled his eyes. "You can say that again. Believe me, I had to live with her growing up."

He told a story of the time Cassandra made him so angry he'd accidentally thrown a baseball bat through a window as they caught up with the girls. It wouldn't take them much longer to reach the bridge. Probably an hour or two after lunch, the kids would be reunited with their mom and everyone would feel a whole lot better.

They were still a good six hours of hiking to where they'd left the cars, so there would probably be one more meal of eating fish and protein bars and whatever other edible plants he and Noah could find, but tonight everyone would be back together and in their own beds.

A flash of bright light reflecting from up on the ridge in front of them caught Tanner's attention, but by the time he could pinpoint where it had come from it was gone. A reflection of that type was almost always from something people had brought with them into the wilderness. Animals did their utmost to blend in. People were the ones who carried items that reflected and drew attention to themselves—binoculars, cameras, cell phones...

Rifle sights.

Seeing other people in this section of the wilderness wasn't completely unusual, although there were much more popular areas for both hiking and rafting. So Tanner wasn't concerned, but he was definitely aware.

When he saw the brief reflection again fifteen minutes later, on par with their location and pace, then he became concerned.

But not overly so. Yes, there were people ahead of them, moving at the same pace as them, and looking over their shoulder to make sure he and Bree and the kids were still moving. But whoever it was couldn't mean them harm, or at least didn't mean to shoot them outright, because they had more than enough opportunity to do it. Their watchers had the higher ground, they were hidden and Tanner was unarmed.

Until there was reason to change the plan, he wasn't going to. Nevertheless, he subtly picked up their pace.

He saw the reflective glimmer one more time before they curved around the ridge and came to the suspension bridge that would lead them over the river and back to safety.

Except the bridge had been destroyed. Pieces of rope and lumber hung in disarray, still attached to the cliff on the other side of the river, but completely removed from their side.

How the hell had that happened?

The bridge had been around as long as Tanner could remember. The river was relatively narrow at this juncture, so the catenary rope bridge had been built across it. The thing had scared him to death the first couple of times he'd crossed it, the way it would sway with each step. It was only as he got older and became more aware of physics and mechanics that he'd come to understand how safe and secure the bridge really was.

Of course, he hadn't been up here in at least two years, so it was possible there'd been some damage before now and Tanner just hadn't realized it.

"Houston, I think we have a problem," Bree muttered. "I hope this isn't the only way across the river."

"No, there are three more bridges farther downriver." And they would go to them—but first he wanted to check this one out. Handing out another protein bar to the kids for them to split, Tanner scooted down so he could get a better look at where the rope bridge had once been secured into the hard rock of the ravine.

When he saw it, he had to swallow his curse.

The bridge itself had definitely been cut by hand. More than cut. It had been completely destroyed. The rings attached to the wall of rock were still solidly embedded, but just beyond the metal the rope had been destroyed. It looked like someone had taken a blowtorch to it.

"Anything interesting?"

The kids were chattering as they continued munching on their bars.

"Definitely wasn't destroyed by mother nature."

Bree helped hoist him back up to ground level. "Why would someone want to destroy a bridge?"

That was the real question, wasn't it? And Tanner had a bad feeling about the answer.

There were three more bridges they could use, but getting to them was going to take them directly through an area that would leave them completely vulnerable, especially if the people who had been tracking them the last couple of hours intended them harm.

"What will Noah and Marilyn do when they get to their side of the bridge and see that it's unusable?"

"Noah knows about the other bridges. There is a secondary base camp five miles from here. If I were him, that's where I'd assume we would go."

Bree had already caught on to the tension in his voice. "Is it time to be concerned yet?"

Was it time to be concerned? At one point in their relationship Tanner would've tried to shelter her, to keep the truth from her. But he'd learned the hard way that wasn't a good idea. Bree could handle herself and was an asset in almost every situation.

He cupped her cheek. "There's no need to panic. And this could all still be coincidence. But yes, there is reason to think it might be time for concern."

Eva walked over to them and stood right next to Bree. "Are we not going to get to see Mommy?" she asked, her little lip quivering.

Bree smiled, but it was tight. "We are, pumpkin. We're just going to need to go to another bridge."

"Hey, Eva, you've been walking a long time. Can I give you a piggyback ride?" Tanner asked with a wink. "Then in a few minutes you can give me one."

The little girl giggled at his silliness and he took the opportunity to swing her up and around on his back. He gave Bree a nod, which she returned, and then looked over at Sam. "You ready to pick up the pace a little bit, champ? If we're going to beat your mom and Noah to the next bridge, we'll have to double-time it."

More like if they were going to make sure they beat the people who were tracking them, but no need to worry the kid with that info.

"Yeah, let's go!" Sam responded.

They walked at a pace faster than they'd been going before, but not fast enough to clue in the people watching them that Tanner was onto them. Bree did a great job keeping the kids talking—about computers, no less—and Tanner kept an eye on the ridge above them as the path they were on started to take them closer to the river's edge once again.

They'd gone about a mile when Tanner saw the light reflected up off the ridge again. When Bree stopped talking for a moment and caught his eye, he realized she'd seen it too. It wasn't until a couple of moments later when he saw a second reflection from the northeastern ridge that he realized they were actually in trouble.

It wasn't one person following them—it was two. At *least* two.

And if Tanner kept them on the path they were walking, they would be moving straight into an area where their followers held all the high ground, and all the advantages. It would make them sitting ducks.

He could be wrong. It could be two sets of hikers just out on their way not even thinking about the reflections their cameras or binoculars were making. It could be hunters up on the ridge, aware of his and the kids' presence but not intending any harm.

But it could also be someone who had already sabotaged their raft and forced their party to separate.

Tanner wasn't willing to take the chance.

There was only one way to know for sure, and that was to lead Bree and the kids deeper into the wilderness.

Catching Bree's eye, he tilted his head to the side and led them off the worn path.

She continued the ongoing conversation with the kids and Tanner didn't discourage it. Their followers were too far away to hear them at this point.

Away from the clearer path the ground was harder to navigate. Tanner would've liked to go much faster, but if somebody twisted an ankle it would definitely slow them down. He hated to add three or four extra miles to an already full day of walking for little legs, but doing this would give whoever was watching them the chance to move on.

Or let Tanner know for certain that they were in trouble.

The kids walked for a while, then Tanner gave Sam a piggyback. Bree, trouper that she was, held Eva for as long as she could, giving the little girl a break. After two miles Tanner swung them back toward the main path again. They walked parallel to it for a good half a mile, and even though he'd kept a close eye out, he didn't see any trace of anyone following them. Maybe he had been paranoid. A good cop was always a little paranoid, and maybe this time it was nothing.

"How are we doing?" Bree asked as the kids walked a few steps ahead of them.

"I haven't seen anything to make me suspicious for the last half a mile. I'm thinking maybe I was a bit overzealous."

She reached over and squeezed his hand. "I like it when you're overzealous. Although generally you're not in the middle of the wilderness when you decide to be."

He wrapped an arm around her shoulder and pulled her up against him, kissing her forehead. "Let's get back on the main path and deliver these kids to their mom."

They were almost to the clearing they would cut through to get back on the main path when Eva let out a disgusted sound.

"Ew. That's so gross."

When Tanner crouched down next to her to see what had gotten her attention, he expected some sort of bug or dead critter. But it wasn't. It was three cigarette butts.

"Mommy says smoking is gross," Eva informed him.

"Do people smoke even out in the woods?" Sam said.

"They do if they're addicted to cigarettes," Bree responded.

Tanner picked up one of the butts, much to the kids' dismay.

"You don't smoke, do you, Lips?" Sam asked.

Tanner brought the butt up to his nose and breathed in. The scent of tobacco was still very present. These butts weren't more than an hour old.

Someone had been sitting here, waiting. No hunter would smoke out in the open like that. It would scare all the prey away. Someone had been waiting for something much more specific.

"Everybody, back into the tree line," Tanner said, pushing them rapidly in that direction. He could tell by the kids' faces that he was making them nervous, but it couldn't be helped.

They were definitely being followed. And he was afraid not just followed...

Hunted.

Chapter Thirteen

Bree grabbed the kids' hands as Tanner led them deep into the thick shelter of the trees.

"I need to go check something out, okay? You guys stay here." He gave both kids a smile and a wink, which encouraged them a little bit, then turned to her. "I'm just going to see what I can find out. Info gathering only."

Obviously, his feeling that he was being paranoid had passed, and it had something to do with those cigarette butts. Someone had been there recently.

She nodded. "We'll be right here getting a little rest in case we need to do more walking."

The kids groaned at the thought of more walking.

"Whatever's left to eat in the backpack, go ahead and do it," Tanner said.

He didn't elaborate, but Bree could read between the lines: get calories into their system in case we need to run.

She nodded. "We'll be fine. You be careful."

With a nod he was gone.

"Bree Cheese, what's happening?" Eva asked.

"I'm not exactly sure, but I think we might be playing a big game of hide-and-seek."

The kids obviously didn't believe her, but they didn't argue. They got out the last two protein bars and began splitting them, wrapping a chunk for Tanner.

With their bellies the slightest bit full, both kids' eyes began to droop. Bree couldn't blame them. They'd already walked at least five miles today. And given what they'd been through in the last twenty-four hours, they probably needed as much rest as they could get.

Bree didn't have that luxury. She kept her eyes open and her ears attuned for any sound of danger. Not that she knew what danger would sound like, or what she would do if an enemy—man or animal—attacked.

When she got back to Risk Peak, she was going to put some concerted effort into researching wilderness survival.

She grimaced. *After* she wrote her wedding vows. First, she had to put her researching abilities into that. Or…maybe whatever was happening right now would drag out to a month and they'd have to cancel the wedding. She and Tanner really could just go in front of the judge. It would solve all her problems.

All her problems except for whatever potential nicotine-riddled danger was out there. Plus, Sam and Eva would be miserable without their mom for that long. And she was sure Marilyn was already beside herself with worry. So she couldn't wish for that.

Tanner came back into their little hiding spot as silently as he'd left, nearly giving Bree a heart attack.

"Damn, you're spooky quiet," she said when she could get a word out. At least the kids were still asleep.

He didn't smile. "We're in trouble."

"For sure?"

He nodded and sat down, grabbing the water and the protein bar. "There are three people waiting for us up ahead. It's definitely a trap. They were waiting for us to pick up the main path again, and then we would've been sitting ducks for whatever they had planned."

"Who? Why?"

"I don't know. Someone from my past or yours? We've certainly found out over the last year that we're not without enemies." He pointed to the kids. "Or somebody attached to Ellis? Maybe he even found a way around his ankle monitor. Ronnie wouldn't have been able to get in touch with us if that happened. I couldn't get close enough to see their faces. All I know is that they were triangulated for a capture another mile and a half down, and we were about to walk right into them."

"So what's the plan?"

"We head deeper into the woods. I've been around this wilderness all my life, so that's an advantage. They're expecting us to show up on the main path in the next hour or two. It will take them a while to figure out we're not coming back that way, after all. That's the second advantage."

He sounded sure of himself. That reassured her. "Okay. Let's do it."

He touched her arm. "But we've also got disadvantages. Two kids who can be pushed physically only so far. No weapons. I could try to take them out myself, but that's risky, and would leave you relatively defenseless if I wasn't successful."

"Not to mention pretty damn lost."

He gave her a half smile that didn't hold much humor. "And as if that's not enough excitement, that storm is rolling in faster than we figured. It's going to hit in the next twenty-four hours."

She squeezed his hand. "Okay, that's a lot of variables to consider. So we try to backtrack our way around them?"

Tanner began packing the water bottle and trash into the backpack. "If we can. I have no idea how skilled they are at tracking. But we'll have to leave as small a trail for them to follow as possible." He shook his head. "It's going to be hard on the kids—scary and stressful. I don't think there's any way around that."

"I told them we were playing a game of hide-and-seek."

He smiled. "From here on out it will have to be as quiet a game of hide-and-seek as we can manage."

They both hated to traumatize these kids any further, but survival trumped everything else. Staying alive was the most important thing.

They woke the kids up and Tanner explained that they were going to do some serious wilderness training. Both kids looked a little skeptical, but Tanner got Sam on board by telling him it was similar to the training Noah had done in the army.

"I don't want to be in the army," Eva whispered to Bree. "I want to play soccer or work on the computer games you gave me. I'm not a soldier."

Bree buttoned up the little girl's jacket; now that it was late afternoon it was getting cooler. "I'm not a soldier either, sweetheart. So we'll just use our brains to help out as much as possible, okay? We'll just keep very quiet and use our eyes and ears to look out for what Tanner is talking about. I know you can do that. You're so good with computers, like your mom."

Eva nodded solemnly.

They moved out in a single-file line.

"Okay, here's the wilderness training game," Tanner said. "We're trying to make it so that nobody can follow us."

"Like hide-and-seek?" Eva asked.

"Yes. A little like hide-and-seek. But also wilderness hide-and-seek. That means we try not to break any branches or step in any soft soil."

"Because soft soil would leave a footprint?" Sam asked.

"For exactly that reason." Tanner beamed at him and the boy was obviously thrilled.

"We walk on rocks, if we can, and stay in a single-file line as much as possible."

Bree's heart swelled in her chest. This man was going to make such a wonderful father. To be so in tune with the danger around them, but calm and mindful of the children's needs also.

The kids were both smiling as they set off in a single-file line, Tanner leading the way and Bree bringing up the rear. Tanner held branches out of the way so that everyone could more easily proceed without them breaking. As he passed by plants that contained something edible, he pointed to it and he and Sam grabbed what they could and put it in the backpack.

The kids held tough for a long time. Longer than most kids their age would have, testament of what they'd survived earlier in their life. But when both of them began tripping, Sam falling and cutting his elbow, Bree knew they were in trouble. There was no way they were going to be able to double back as far as Tanner wanted. The kids weren't going to last that long.

The sun was beginning to set, making it even more difficult to see in the thick woods.

Tanner called them to a halt, and they began drinking from the canteen they'd refilled at the stream they'd crossed a mile or two back.

All the miles were beginning to blend together for Bree; she couldn't imagine what it was like for the kids. And yet they didn't complain.

She looked up from sipping her water and found Tanner studying her.

"Circling back is not going to work tonight. It's too far."

She nodded. At this point she wasn't even sure *she* could make it, much less the kids.

"Do we have a plan B?"

He grimaced and nodded. "We get deeper in and find somewhere to hide until they pass."

The kids were listening intently, but there was no way to hide this from them, not anymore.

"Stranger danger?" Eva whispered.

"Yes," Tanner smiled at her. "Unfortunately, we've got some stranger danger. We need to hide and rest for a while. We'll let them pass, then go a different route home."

"What about Mom?" Sam asked.

"Noah will get her home. He'll be waiting for us with your mom. Both of them will be so happy to see us when we get there," Bree said.

"I'll carry both of them, if you get the backpack," Tanner said.

Bree shook her head. "There's no way you can carry both of them and continue to hide our tracks. I'll piggyback Miss Eva and you give Sam a ride."

"I can walk," Sam said. "I'm not a baby."

"I'm not a baby either," Eva said with a pout.

"Nobody's a baby," Tanner said, cutting them off. "We need to move as quickly as possible, with as few steps as possible. So if you happen to be the two shortest people here, then you get a piggyback ride. But listen, this is a wilderness piggyback. That means you need to hold on and help as much as possible with your legs and arms. Okay?"

They both nodded. Tanner walked over and cupped

the back of Bree's neck. "You're going to have to dig deep, freckles. We need to move fast and find the best shelter we can get."

"I can take it."

He kissed her hard. "I know you can. Let's go."

Tanner hoisted Sam up onto his back, and Bree did the same with Eva.

Tanner hadn't been lying. He set a brutal pace, not slowing even as they headed uphill, over rocky terrain or through thick underbrush.

Bree forced herself to keep pace even when her lungs felt like they were on fire and she had stitches in both sides of her waist. Eva did what she could to help, keeping her legs hooked around Bree's hips and holding a lot of her own weight much of the time. But it was still agonizing.

Tanner periodically turned around to check on her but never offered to stop. That didn't make her angry. It meant he trusted her to do what had to get done.

But she hoped he was listening out for any trouble, because, honestly, someone could walk right up on her and she'd never hear them over the sound of her own labored breathing.

It was pitch-black by the time they stopped. Bree could barely see two feet in front of her.

"This," he said. She got a tiny bit of satisfaction to hear that Tanner was breathing hard too. "This is probably as best a place we're going to find. Everybody stay right here, and I'm going to make sure there's nothing living inside."

Inside what? Bree had no idea. Tanner took a sip

from the canteen, then handed it to Bree before disappearing into the darkness. She grabbed Eva's and Sam's hands just to make sure she didn't lose them in the darkness.

"What is Lips doing?" Sam asked.

"He's finding a safe place for us to rest. He'll be back in just a second." She prayed that was true, because she had no idea what she was going to do if she suddenly became the adult in charge.

But he was back just a few moments later. "Okay, no critters. At least, not now. We're safe to go in."

"In what?" Bree asked. "A cave?"

"It's really more of an overhang than an actual cave, but it's sheltered on three sides and can fit all four of us."

Tanner led them forward and down a small hill. The moon was finally coming out, so she could just barely make out the shape of the natural shelter he'd found. But he was right, it should keep them hidden for the most part.

"We can't make a fire," Tanner whispered. "So we're all going to need to huddle together with the blankets to keep warm. We'll have to eat whatever we collected on the way. But most important, we're going to have to be as still and quiet as possible, okay?"

The kids nodded. If they weren't too scared, they'd probably be out like a light as soon as they ate.

Tanner gave them all some more water and they got out the food they'd been collecting along the way today. The temperature was dropping now that it was dark, so Bree had the kids go ahead and wrap themselves in the blanket. Tanner ate a little, then whispered that he would be back in a few minutes.

"Where is he going?" Eva asked, worry evident in her little voice.

"Just to get something we need. He'll be right back." Bree didn't know exactly what Tanner was doing, but she knew her words were true.

Sure enough, he was back a few minutes later, two sticks in his hand. He laid them both by Bree.

"This is as close as I can get to weapons. Obviously, they're not going to be super useful against… more modern weaponry." She appreciated that he didn't say the word *gun* in front of the kids. No need to plant that in their minds right before they were stuck in the dark all night. "But it's something. Use it like a baseball bat. If someone who's not me comes in here, make your first shot count."

His giving her pointers on how to best use that large stick as a weapon was scaring her more than anything else he'd said today. Because he really thought she was going to have to use it.

But now wasn't the time to give in to panic. Tanner needed her to be strong. So she just reached over, found his hand in the dark and squeezed. "Okay."

As she'd predicted, it didn't take long for the kids to fall asleep. It was dark, they couldn't talk and there was nothing to see, not to mention their little bodies had been pushed hard today.

Once they were, Tanner brought his lips all the way to her ear and spoke quietly. "I'm going out. This place is good as a shelter, but if they find us here, we are basically sitting ducks. At least from out there if someone finds you, I can do something about it."

She nodded so he would know she understood.

"If I can take one or more out, I'm going to try to do that."

She stiffened. They undoubtedly had weapons. And he didn't know how many of them there were.

His hand came up and threaded into her hair on the other side of her head, the motion so Tanner-like and in control that it helped calm her.

"These guys have guns. They're dangerous, freckles—I can feel it in my gut. If I don't come back, at first light, you take the kids and run."

She shook her head frantically. There was no way she was leaving him.

"Yes." His fingers gripped her hair more firmly. "You go in the morning. You follow the direction the sun is rising until you run into the river, then turn right and follow the river south all the way until you hit the road. You get Noah, Whitaker, Ronnie… *everybody*. You send them all back up to help me."

"I don't want to leave you," she whispered.

"I'm going to be there for our wedding, don't you worry. But you have to promise me you'll go. I can keep myself alive, but I can't watch them hurt you or those kids."

"If you're not at the wedding, I'm going to make you wait another whole year to get married, with the no-touching rule still in effect," she lied. She'd never be able to live that long without touching him.

He kissed her forehead. "You can damn well bet I'm not going to miss our wedding night—you've got too many dirty debts to pay. I'll see you soon, freckles."

With a hard kiss on her lips, he disappeared silently into the darkness.

Chapter Fourteen

Tanner moved as silently as possible through the trees, stopping every so often to try to listen for anything out of place. Noah was so much better at this than he was. But to keep Bree and the kids safe, he would damn well learn how to do it fast.

He heard a soft bit of radio static crackle from a distance and knew it was the men signaling to one another. The good news was they were at a distance, nowhere near him or the hideout. The bad news was these guys were communicating via walkie-talkie.

And they were definitely around, and they were prepared.

Moving as silently as he could, Tanner made rounds farther and farther out from the hiding spot. He knew the men were out here, but he didn't want to stumble on one of them unaware.

What was the best plan? Try to lead them away? Would Bree run with the kids like he told her?

She would. If he didn't come back for one reason or another, he had to believe she would.

He shut his eyes again, focusing on the sounds

around him. He heard the soft static again and moved silently in that direction. When he heard it again many minutes later he froze. That time it had been close. Way too close. He remained still. This might be his chance to take one of the men out.

He kept himself motionless to listen and figure out what direction he'd need to move, but this time it was voices that caught his attention.

"How many times are you going to let that damn thing give off noise?"

Tanner froze. That voice. He knew that voice. Where from?

"As many times as I have to until you all agree they might've moved on."

"They had two small children, no supplies, no food, no light. It made much more sense for them to stop once it got dark. So we keep searching around here, Paul."

Damn it, how did Tanner know that voice? He took a few steps to the side. If he was going to try to take both of them out, he would have to come from the best vantage point possible.

"Well, I've searched my quadrant twice, and there's nobody there," Paul hissed. "No sign of anyone. I think they moved on."

"If it wasn't for you and your damn cigarettes, we would've had them back near the trail."

Paul let out a curse. "I wanted to have a cigarette break. And how do you know they found them?"

"Well, they turned in a different direction and

started covering up their tracks at that clearing where they obviously found your butts."

The voice clicked into place in Tanner's mind. It was Oscar Stobbart, Jared's lawyer.

"Shut the hell up, Oscar. You don't know for sure it was my cigarettes that tipped them off."

"And anyway," Paul continued. "That bitch isn't even with them. We're not going to be able to bring her back to Jared if she isn't anywhere around."

"I'll admit, I didn't expect her to get in a different raft from her kids. She hasn't been five feet away from those brats for weeks," Oscar whispered. "If she hadn't separated from them, we could've taken them all at once. That tiny detonator was pretty effective."

Tanner took a couple steps closer so he could hear their low voices more clearly. He wasn't surprised at all to hear they'd sabotaged the raft.

"We work on the kids now and get them to Jared. It won't take much to get Marilyn to fall in line once they're gone."

"But what about the adults?" Paul said. "Jared doesn't want the kids hurt, but I've got the taste for a little hunting."

"The man is a cop," Oscar hissed. "It was one thing when we were just going to take out some woman. It's another thing to bring the entire police force of Colorado down on us."

"You worry too much. Always have. It's the wilderness. Accidents happen in the wilderness all the time. Even to cops."

"Right now, we stick to the plan. We can't get Marilyn, but we can get the kids."

"Fine," Paul said. "But if the cop or the woman poses a threat, I won't hesitate to do what needs to be done."

Tanner had to take them out now. Once they split up again the chances of him finding them both were slim. If he could eliminate these two, their odds of escaping the third were at least better.

Oscar and Paul both had weapons, but Tanner had the element of surprise. Even if he could take only one of them out, that would give Bree and the kids a better chance.

It was worth the risk.

He crouched, muscles flexing, about to spring, when he was tackled from the side and thrown into a tree.

"What was that?" Paul said.

Tanner couldn't say a word at all; fingers were pressed up against his windpipe, completely cutting off his ability to make any sound.

"Quiet, Hot Lips, it's me," Noah whispered into his ear.

Tanner stopped all struggle, and Noah immediately released his hold on Tanner's throat.

"We need to take them," Tanner whispered. "They're planning—"

Noah gave a sharp shake of his head. "Setup," he said in the lowest of voices.

Tanner kept completely still and silent. Noah

knew something he obviously didn't. They waited there for what seemed like forever.

"It didn't work," said a third voice, one Tanner hadn't heard yet and had had no idea was around. "They must really not be anywhere around here. Otherwise the cop would've made a play. Trying to take you guys out would've been the smartest thing to do."

"It was worth a try. Let's split back up and make another round," Oscar said. "I still hold that they wouldn't have kept going with the kids. Too hard."

The other two men agreed and in a few moments there was silence once again as they faded back into the wilderness.

Tanner forced himself to count to five hundred before he even began to move, but once again Noah stopped him with a silent shake of the head and a hand on his shoulder.

Tanner was almost to a thousand this time before Noah finally moved.

"Being extra cautious?" Tanner whispered.

"There's a fourth, who was hanging behind just in case. I don't know where he was, but he was out there."

His brother was damn spooky sometimes.

"Are you sure there's nobody out there now?" Tanner whispered.

"Not near here. They're resuming their search."

"I'm pretty sure you just saved my life, so thanks."

Noah squeezed his shoulder. "Let's move. I've got to pick something up before we go to wherever you stashed Bree and the kids."

"Pick something up?" Tanner whispered. "Like a pizza?" Although, damn, pizza sounded good.

"Indefinitely more frustrating than pizza, trust me."

They made their way north, away from the hideout, but Tanner didn't question. Noah had a reason for whatever he was doing. Noah always had a reason.

"Did you track us?"

"Yeah. Damn near impossible to hide two kids and an inexperienced hiker, although you did a good job." His voice was so low Tanner could hardly hear him, and he was right next to him. "Tracking these guys was easier. I would've been here much sooner."

Tanner waited for him to finish the sentence but evidently it was complete in Noah's mind.

They walked for another five minutes, definitely not in a straight line. Then they came to an outcropping of rocks near a small drop-off by a waterfall. Tanner had no idea what they were doing there, until a blur of white jumped out at them, stick in hand.

Tanner jumped out of the way, but Noah was obviously expecting it. He spun around, ducking from where the branch would've clobbered him in the head, and behind their attacker.

"Whoa there, tiger," he whispered, grabbing the attacker by the waist from behind and spinning her around.

"Noah?"

It was Marilyn. She lowered the stick, then looked between the two men.

"Tanner? Where are the kids?"

Tanner turned to his brother. "This is the *pizza*?"

"Like I said, more frustrating than a pizza. She followed me. We sent Francis and Barb home when we saw the bridge was out. Marilyn was supposed to go with them, but somebody is not great at following directions."

"I don't give a damn about your directions when my kids' lives are at stake," Marilyn spit out.

It was the most words, and definitely the most anger, Tanner had ever seen out of the quiet woman.

She turned to him. "Are they okay? We saw them fall out of the raft, but Noah assured me that the flares meant you guys were unharmed."

"We were. We are." He caught his brother's eyes in the dim light. "We survived the rafting accident with no problem. But we've got much bigger issues now."

The sound of the water covered most of their talking. "Your raft was sabotaged, wasn't it?" Noah asked.

"How did you know?"

"Found something similar on ours. Some sort of puncture mechanism on a timer. I don't know if it malfunctioned or if they only ever planned on taking down one raft."

Tanner muttered a curse.

"We would've gotten here a lot sooner," Noah continued, "but they took out not only the first bridge but the next two also."

"You must've been hauling ass the whole day to have gotten here by now."

Noah shrugged and turned to Marilyn. "It's Jared."

Even in the darkness Tanner could see the tension bolt through the woman. "He's here?"

"He's not here himself," Tanner said. "But I know for sure one of the men tracking us is Oscar Stobbart. The other guy's name was Paul. I'm assuming that's Paul Wyn."

Marilyn seemed to shrink inside herself. "I—I…"

Noah pulled her up against his chest. "Concentrate on what you know that might be able to help us right now. Leave the rest for another time. What do we need to know about these guys?"

She sucked in a couple of deep breaths. "They'll do anything for one another. I think Jared might've had something to do with Paul's wife's death, but I could never prove it."

Tanner barely refrained from rolling his eyes. "They're obviously used to working together."

"Where are the kids? Are they hurt? Scared? I just want to get to them."

"They're hidden with Bree. Sleeping. They're not hurt and have been absolute troupers today. They're hidden pretty well right now, but I don't want to leave them any longer than necessary. I was going to try to take out our hunters, but that was when I thought I was taking on two."

"We need a plan," Noah said.

Tanner nodded. "Let's get back to Bree. I know

she's worried sick. And then, yeah, a plan. Which probably involves us splitting up."

Noah gave him a nod. Neither of them liked the thought of splitting their defenses, but the most important thing right now was making sure to get those kids back safe. Out of Jared Ellis's clutches.

Chapter Fifteen

Every noise made by an animal, the break of a twig or even the leaves shifting in the wind sounded like desperate danger to Bree. She had long since placed herself in the mouth of their little overhang, determined to be a buffer between menace and these kids.

Whoever was hunting them might find them here, but they damn well weren't going to touch Eva and Sam without Bree getting a few good bashes in.

She refused to even think about Tanner not coming back, even when minute after minute marched closer to dawn and he still didn't return. Tanner was a hero; it was what he did by trade. But she didn't want him to be a hero tonight. She wanted him to come back and hide with her and find a way out of this by sneaking off in the dark, rather than facing the enemy head-on.

A silent tear ran down her cheek before she could stop it. Tanner's propensity for facing the enemy head-on was one of the reasons she'd fallen in love with him. But now she just wanted him back safe in her arms.

With every second she willed him closer until finally he was there right in front of her, crawling into the cave.

The branch shook in her hand and she swallowed a sob.

"I'm okay, freckles." His lips were on hers in a brief, hard kiss, then he scooted closer in next to her.

Two more people climbed in behind him. Bree couldn't believe it when she saw Marilyn and Noah.

Marilyn barely paid any attention to her, just crawled frantically past her to see the kids. The soft sobs coming from the woman were nothing less than heartbreaking. Quiet kissing noises filled the small space.

"Mommy?" Eva's sleepy voice said.

"Shh. I'm here. Go back to sleep."

"We played hide-and-seek. Soldier style."

"You can tell me all about it soon," Marilyn whispered.

In the darkness, Bree could barely make out Marilyn cuddling both kids to her.

"How did you find us?" Bree asked Noah.

"I had planned on tracking you, but Tanner did a pretty good job hiding those tracks. So I ended up tracking the guys hunting you. They weren't being nearly as careful."

"It's Jared Ellis's buddies," Tanner said. "I overheard them. They're after the kids."

"We need to get out of here, as soon as possible," Noah whispered. "Split up. They're not sure where you are right now, but they'll find you eventually."

"I'll lead them in the wrong direction. Give them just enough clues to have something to follow, then lose them when the storm hits," Tanner said. "You take Marilyn, Bree and the kids and get them to safety."

"You sure that's the best play?" Noah asked.

"I think it might be our only play. I can't justify leaving a trail of dead bodies when we don't know for sure what their purpose is and they haven't made any overt attempts on our life."

Tanner turned to Marilyn. "Their endgame is to bring you and the kids to Jared, right? Not to kill anyone?"

"He doesn't want to kill me. Even the last time when he put me in the hospital, I don't think he intended to kill me. And the kids have always been more of a means to an end to control me. Otherwise Jared mostly ignored them. But you guys... I don't know if they'll hurt you."

Noah turned to Tanner. "Why don't I lead the bad guys into the wilderness, and *you* take the merry gang back to town."

Tanner shook his head. "Because if they do come after you guys, I want you to use your skills and take them out. I'm handy with a gun, but I don't have the hand-to-hand combat skills you do. I'm not sure I'll be able to protect them the way you would. Better for me to be the decoy."

"I'm not letting you go alone," Bree interjected. "You're going to need more than one person if you're trying to fool them into thinking there're still four of us traveling through the wilderness."

"She's right, you know," Noah said. "They won't buy the ruse for long with you by yourself."

"I don't like it," Tanner finally said.

It was probably a good thing he couldn't see her roll her eyes in the dark. "You don't have to like it, you just have to do it."

Noah gave a low chuckle. "Consider it practice for marriage."

Silence from Tanner.

"I don't like it," he finally said again. "I don't know that I can protect you."

"I don't need you to protect me anymore. You've been teaching me how to do that for myself since I've known you." She squeezed his hand. "We protect each other."

It was a testament to how far they'd come, how much Tanner now really looked at her as a partner in all areas of life—even the scary parts—that he finally muttered a soft agreement.

Noah slid toward the overhang entrance. "I'm going to go find a clear path for us. Try to get a bead on where they are searching now. I'll lead them farther out if I can. I'll be back in one hour. Be ready to move. That's when they're most likely to stop for a rest and we're going to use it to our advantage."

Without another word he was gone. Tanner looped his arm around Bree's shoulders and pulled her against him until his lips were at her temple. "You stubborn thing. I'm planning on all sorts of payback on our wedding night."

"It's a deal."

"Try to get a little rest before Noah comes back. We're going to have to move hard once he does."

She didn't think there was any way she would be able to sleep, but she scooted back toward Marilyn, who was hugging both her kids to her.

"Bree," Marilyn whispered. "I'm so sorry I brought this into your life."

"Don't even start with me. I'm thankful every day you are in my life. No one is to blame for Jared and his cronies except Jared and his cronies. So don't talk like that. Let's escape, get Jared thrown back in jail and get my wedding over with."

"You do know you just listed marrying the man you love as part of a series of traumatic events."

Bree wasn't facing Marilyn, and probably couldn't have seen her face even if she was this far back in the shelter, but she could hear her friend's smile.

"Just the saying my vows part. Maybe running for my life will knock something loose and I'll be able to get them written."

She meant to say more, but the next thing Bree knew, Tanner was shaking her awake. Bree hadn't even realized she'd fallen asleep.

"It's time to go."

Noah was back. He was breathing heavy and drinking water from the canteen.

"I've got us a window open with them, led one

of them in the opposite direction. We need to take advantage of it."

Marilyn woke up Sam and started talking softly to him. A moment later the little boy walked over to Noah.

Marilyn picked up the sleeping Eva in her arms. "We're ready. She'll wake up, but she'll keep quiet."

"That storm coming in is going to be worse than we thought," Noah told Tanner. "And it's going to hit soon."

"Good. We'll use it to our advantage."

"Go back toward the waterfall," Noah said. "It gives you multiple exit options. Once you're there, let out a scream or something to get them headed that way."

The two brothers hugged briefly, and Bree hugged Marilyn.

"Be careful," Tanner said. "They may not all come after us."

"We all better be back in time to be standing at that wedding, or Mom and Cassandra both are gonna kill us."

"Trust me, I know," Tanner muttered.

Less than a minute later they were all out of the shelter heading in different directions. Noah had Sam on his back and Marilyn was carrying Eva.

For them, stealth was more important than speed, at least right now.

Tanner grabbed Bree's hand, moving as quickly and silently as possible through the forest. He stopped every once in a while to listen, once completely changing directions, but it wasn't long before they made it to a small waterfall. They filled their canteen and caught their breath.

"This is it," Tanner said. "You ready to lead them in this direction? There's no turning back after this."

Was she ready? Was anybody ever actually *ready* to bring people with weapons hunting them in their direction?

She nodded. She knew the plan.

"Make it count. We want to make sure they hear."

Tanner kissed her, then stepped back.

Bree screamed.

Chapter Sixteen

Tanner never wanted to hear that sound from Bree again. She screamed his name like she was terrified out of her mind.

Which she may be, although she certainly hadn't shown any sign of breaking.

He kissed her again to stop the scream, then grabbed her hand. "Let's go."

They started pushing themselves almost unbearably hard. He could hear Bree's breaths behind him, sawing in and out, but she didn't complain, and he didn't stop. But after a couple of miles, they finally slowed.

These first few miles were critical. They had to get enough distance not to be caught, but not go so fast that the hunters figured out they were the decoys, not whom they really wanted.

But most important, they needed to provide Noah and Marilyn a chance to get back to safety.

They continued to move as the sun came up. They didn't speak, not knowing how far away the trackers might be. Tanner left very deliberate clues at first— ones they would have to be blind to miss.

They went deeper and deeper into the wilderness. If the men hunting them were as familiar with this area as he was, that would've been an instant clue that something was awry. It would be stupid to lead the children deeper into the wilderness with no supplies and a storm coming. At what point would that thought cross their minds? Would Noah have enough time to get Marilyn and the kids to safety?

Now that it was daylight, he and Bree had to move much more carefully, staying in the cover of the trees. If they went too much out in the open, they might be spotted with binoculars, or even worse, a rifle scope.

Like Marilyn had said, Jared wanted her and the kids alive, but anyone else might be considered expendable.

By midafternoon their energy was starting to fail. They ate some berries and drank water everywhere they could, but the calories they were getting into their bodies were nowhere near their output. That would begin to take a toll quickly.

Bree was amazing—not that he'd had much doubt she would be. She didn't complain, not even once. Not when he looked back and she was pale or sweating. She just kept pushing even when it got harder and harder.

The hunters were gaining on them. They had nourishment and equipment he and Bree didn't have.

Tanner wasn't exactly sure when they'd spotted him and Bree, but there was no doubt they had. The good news was they were still following, so that meant they must think the kids were still with them. The bad news was…everything else. No food or weapons, and moving farther from help with each step.

Noah would be back with the assistance they needed. Tanner just had to buy him more time.

A quiet cry fell from Bree's lips as she stumbled on the uneven ground and crashed hard onto her knees, barely catching herself before her face hit the ground. Tanner couldn't even move fast enough to stop her.

He let out a low curse. "We've got to stop. This is game over if one of us breaks a leg," he whispered.

"Where are they? They are still following us, right?"

"Yes, but it's harder for me to tell exactly where they are. The sun isn't shining so brightly, so I'm not catching any reflections off their scopes like I was yesterday. But then again, they're not exactly trying to hide, so I catch a glimpse of one of them every once in a while. Last time was over an hour ago."

He kept his voice low because over an hour ago was an eternity when you were talking about hunting someone in the forest. They could be much closer now.

"So we need to keep going." Exhaustion skirted across her face. She struggled to push herself back up into a standing position, but her movements were jerky and uncoordinated.

Damn it, she was more tired than she'd let on.

He sat down beside her and pulled her down next to him.

"I thought we needed to go? That they are gaining on us." But she didn't try to get back up.

He scooted down next to her and tucked them both up against the tree.

"No, rest for a while. At some point we need to turn back toward civilization."

She closed her eyes. "Have we given them enough time?"

The fact that she was asking that rather than demanding they continue to push forward told Tanner what he needed to know. Bree was getting awful darn close to her breaking point.

Mentally and emotionally she could keep pushing herself. She'd proved that over and over since he'd met her. But the body could go only as far as it could go.

"Quit looking at me like that," she said without opening her eyes.

"Looking at you like what? And how can you tell anything anyway if your eyes are closed?"

"I can tell just by the way you're breathing."

His eyebrow rose. "All right, smarty, exactly how am I looking at you, then?"

"Like you know I want to go on, but my body isn't going to make it."

Damned if that wasn't *exactly* what he was thinking.

"We can't keep going at this pace." He reached over and kissed her temple.

Now those green eyes opened. "But we can for another few hours. Give them the time they need to make sure they're out safely. My body will do whatever I tell it to. And if I tell it it's going hard for another few hours, that's what it's going to do."

Tanner sighed. "I'm sure that's true right up to the point where your body completely collapses. We don't want to let it get to that point."

But he knew they needed to get moving again.

And then it began to rain.

Storms in the Colorado wilderness weren't to be messed with at any time, and this one was a doozy. Rain was pelting them by the time he helped her to her feet a minute later.

"Hopefully this will work in our favor," he told her.

It would certainly make them less visible and might make the hunters stop altogether. They didn't know Tanner knew who they were. He may not have enough to arrest them—what he'd seen and heard had been minimal, and circumstantial—but he damn well wouldn't be taking his eyes off Jared Ellis or any of his posse for as long as needed. They would slip up, and Tanner would be there to take them down when they did.

But right now, they needed to survive this damn wilderness.

They began moving forward again at a slower pace this time, because no matter what Bree said, there was only so much her smaller body could handle.

They tried to keep out of the cold rain as much as

possible, dashing from point to point under anything that would offer them shelter. But it still didn't take long before they were completely soaked.

The only good news was that the farther they went, the less Tanner saw any sign of the hunters.

As lightning lit up the late-afternoon sky, he prayed it was because they'd done the smart thing and chosen to wait out the storm. Of course, the storm was probably going to last another ten hours, but he doubted the men knew that. By the time they did, Noah would definitely have made it back to Risk Peak.

As the wind picked up and began whipping through the trees, Tanner knew they were going to have to find shelter themselves.

A quick look at Bree confirmed it. Her teeth were chattering, lips starting to turn a little blue, despite their exertion. He needed to get her someplace where they could stop, allow themselves time to dry off and raise their body temperatures. He knew just the place and would bet anything the hunters weren't aware of it.

They were almost back to the river. His original plan had been to cut back up the river, leading away from town. But not anymore. He and Bree had bought Noah and Marilyn and the kids plenty of time. If he knew his brother, he'd already gotten Marilyn and the kids to old man Henrikson's house. That old goat was the only person Tanner knew who disliked people more than Noah did. But he had a damn impressive collection of shotguns. And his place would be the first they'd come across on their way into town. Noah would be borrowing a couple of those shotguns his way back out here. The rest of the cavalry would be right behind him.

"Is the storm getting louder?" Bree asked as they stopped to catch their breath by a clump of trees. Right now, Tanner was playing a game of choose your enemy. Hanging out under the trees was a bad idea because of the storm, but they provided them cover from the hunters. Getting away from the trees would be better to avoid the lightning but might make them visible to the people with guns.

"No, that's the river. It's about twenty yards ahead of us, then about ten or fifteen feet straight down over the ledge."

"The same river you told me to run toward this morning with the kids if you didn't make it back?"

"Yep, although you would've hit it about three miles downstream and that's much closer to town."

Her mouth tightened at the thought of having extra miles to walk, he was sure, but she didn't say anything.

"Don't worry, we're not walking the whole way right now. It's time to get out of the storm."

Walking down by the riverbank would be easier but would put them in a weakened tactical position. If one of the hunters came up on the ridge, they'd have a clear shot at them even though the ridge wasn't very high here. They'd have to be doubly careful.

"Okay, let's—"

Tanner felt the burn in his upper arm at the same

time the shot rang out. He and Bree were diving to the ground as a second shot exploded in the tree next to them. Those weren't rifle shots or Tanner would be dead right now. They were from a handgun. That explained why Tanner was still alive—rifles were a hell of a lot more accurate—but it also meant somebody was much closer than he'd expected.

And it also just changed all the rules of the game. Anything Tanner did now would be considered self-defense.

But that fact wouldn't help them if they were dead.

"Are you okay? Are you shot?" Bree began patting him all over his torso.

"Just a graze on my arm. I'm okay. But we've got to move right now."

"Okay."

He grabbed her hand with his, keeping his eye out for the shooter. "We're going to have to split up. Stay down and crawl toward the river. I think it's only one of them, or we'd already be in a lot more trouble."

Bree nodded and began crawling in the direction she needed to go.

Tanner doubled back toward where the gunfire had come from, ignoring the pain in his arm. He could move it, and it wasn't bleeding too much, so treating it would have to wait. Hopefully the rain had muffled the gunshot enough that it wouldn't bring the shooter's buddies into the area.

Tanner kept low and moved in a zigzagging motion, trying to make himself as hard a target to hit as possible.

But he was also moving blind, since he didn't know exactly where the shooter was.

Tanner let out a curse when another shot rang out. Near the water. Near Bree. The bastard had somehow circled back behind him.

He gave up all pretense of hiding or weaving and bolted toward where he'd sent Bree.

"Bree, stay down!" He yelled the words, hoping to redirect the danger back to himself. At least then it wouldn't be pointed at her.

He spotted the shooter at the very edge of the riverbank's cliff. The shooter was facing to the side, away from Tanner, gun pointed at something ahead of him on the ground. It didn't take a genius to figure out it was Bree in front of him, staying low the way Tanner had told her.

The guy was going to shoot her.

Tanner forced every ounce of energy into his legs and rushed as fast as he could toward the man with the gun, praying he'd reach the shooter in time.

Chapter Seventeen

A shot rang out over her head and Bree realized she was going to die.

It wasn't the first time she'd felt that way today. There'd been half a dozen times as they'd run like fiends through the wilderness that she was pretty sure she would either fall over and crack her spine, have a massive coronary from the exertion or step on some creature who decided it didn't like being stepped on and would make its displeasure known by poisoning her.

But this guy staring down the gun at her definitely left little doubt in her mind that she was, in fact, going to die.

"And here I thought I wasn't going to get to do anything interesting," the man said with a smirk.

At least that was what she thought he said, as it was nearly impossible to hear him over the storm and the river barreling below them. As he spoke, she got into a crouching position, trying to think of something to say, something she could barter with, but nothing came to her exhausted mind. She wiped the rain from her eyes and got a good look at the man for the first time.

"You. You're the paramedic from the night of the fire."

"Yep, and things could've gone much easier if you'd just left those two brats with me. That's why we started the fire to begin with. To get them or Marilyn outside. But then that entire damn town showed up."

She leaped to the side while he was talking, knowing it wasn't going to be enough, that he'd still have an easy shot.

But the shot never came.

Instead, Bree watched, first relieved when Tanner crashed into the man, knocking them both to the side and the guy's gun out of his hand, then in horror as the momentum kept them moving forward and over the side of the ravine.

"Tanner!" Bree screamed, scrambling forward to get to him. But both men had already fallen into the water below by the time she got there. The ridge wasn't very high at this point, like Tanner had said—maybe fifteen feet. But how deep was the water? It was flowing pretty quickly, but she couldn't tell how deep it was. In the rain it was difficult to see either man.

When Tanner's head burst through the surface, Bree let out a sob of relief. He was alive. She looked along the ridge for a way to get down to him as he fought to make his way to the river's edge. Every stroke seemed like a struggle for him. Unlike when they'd capsized in the raft, Tanner didn't have on a life jacket. Waterlogged clothes and shoes were dragging him under.

She pushed herself to her feet. In the rain, she would've completely missed the guy's gun if she hadn't literally stepped on it. She knew only a little about handguns, based on what Tanner had taught her the last few months, but any weapon was better than nothing. She tried to keep an eye on him as she ran parallel to the river, looking for any way to get down.

Panic ate like acid through her gut when she finally had to take her eyes off Tanner to find a way down from the ridge. How was she ever going to find him again? She finally found an overhang of rocks and slid and jumped down them as fast as she could, ignoring the burning cuts on her palms as her skin tore on the jagged edges.

"Hang on, baby. Hang on." She said the words over and over as she reached the riverbank and began sprinting back toward Tanner, cursing when she couldn't get enough speed out of her body.

Thunder crackled heavily overhead, lightning immediately flashing in the storm-darkened sky. Vaguely she wondered if the storm would kill them both, even if she could get to Tanner.

The longer she ran, the more panicked she became. Had she somehow missed him? Had he not been able to make it over to the edge? There wasn't any riverbank here, so she was forced to walk in the water. The air seemed to be sucked out of her lungs from the cold, and she was in only six inches of water. How could Tanner have survived completely immersed in the water?

She pressed forward, harder, drawing on energy from her innermost center. Tanner needed her. She had to get to him.

She rounded a small ledge and let out a sob of relief when she saw Tanner standing at the edge of the water. He was swaying almost drunkenly, his big body tilted at an odd angle, his shoulder held awkwardly.

He made some sort of jerky movement, shifting to the side clumsily, and Bree realized the paramedic guy was right behind him. They were fighting. Or…trying to fight. The awkward, stiff movements Tanner was making were definitely not the complex fighting maneuvers she knew he was capable of.

She winced as the paramedic got a solid hook into Tanner's jaw. Tanner stumbled to the side but didn't go down. His left arm still held awkwardly at an angle to his side, Tanner got his own punch in.

Bree kept moving toward them, not wanting to call out and distract Tanner. After another couple of minutes and a few more exhausted punches from both sides, it became evident Tanner was going to triumph.

She was almost to Tanner when his last brutal uppercut to the paramedic's chin sent the man flying back and into the water. He probably would've drowned, but Tanner grabbed him with his good hand and dragged him to the shore, leaving him.

The relief she felt at seeing him alive, and the other man unconscious, wiped the last strength she had, almost causing her to collapse in the water. She slowed to a walk, the fifteen yards she was from Tanner seeming like a mile. She yelled to him, but he couldn't hear her over the storm.

He was looking up at the ridge, and she realized he was looking for her. She called out to him, her voice sounding weak even to her own ears, and he turned. The relief she saw in his eyes, the way his posture relaxed to know that she was alive and unharmed filled her heart almost to bursting.

She stumbled toward him, her own movements jerky with cold and fatigue. She felt like she would never be warm again. She couldn't imagine what Tanner felt like with his body still submerged to midthigh.

Then the whole world seemed to turn black in front of her as the man behind Tanner got to his feet, a huge branch in his hand, held up like a club.

She opened her mouth to scream a warning to Tanner but knew he couldn't hear her. And it would come too late. She did the only thing she could—swung up the gun in her hand and pointed it in the man's direction.

But to Tanner it had to look like she was pointing it directly at him.

His face blanched, but then without her having to explain the plan, without her even knowing what the plan could be, he dropped like a rock into the water, giving her a clear shot of her target.

Tanner trusted her.

Bree didn't hesitate. She squeezed the trigger gently twice the way he'd taught her, aiming for the paramedic's chest—the largest mass.

Surprise lit his face as the force of the shots propelled him backward.

He took one more step forward before falling facedown into the water, the river carrying him away. Bree ignored him, moving as quickly as she could over to Tanner, who was struggling to regain his footing in the water.

She'd killed a man. She would have to deal with that later. Because unless she got them somewhere where they could dry off and warm up, there was going to be more than just one dead body.

She worked herself around to Tanner's less-injured side. Close up, she realized just how much worse his injuries were than she'd realized. His arm was definitely dislocated, but there was also a gash on his head and his face was chalk white.

She stuffed the gun into the waistband of her jeans as she wrapped her arm around Tanner's hips when he staggered. "We've got to get you somewhere you can get dry and warm."

He didn't argue. Couldn't even seem to find the strength to say anything, just nodded.

What was the best plan? Downstream toward the town? But what about the other hunters? They had to have heard all the gunfire and could show up any moment. How many bullets were left in the gun she had? She fought down her panic at not knowing what to do.

"Up—up bridge." His words were so jerky she almost couldn't understand them.

"You want us to go upriver? That's farther away from help."

"Shelter." He was already swaying on his feet. "Sh-shelter by bridge."

She moved directly in front of him, cupping his cheeks with her hands, looking deep into his eyes. It would've been romantic if they both weren't freezing, and he wasn't injured, and she hadn't killed somebody, and other people weren't still hunting them. Romantic.

"Tanner, I need to make sure you're lucid. If you send us upriver and there's nothing there…"

"Shelter. Trust."

She did trust him the same way he'd just trusted her rather than stop and ask why the heck she was pointing a gun at him. He would've been dead if he'd done that.

He knew these woods. He knew where they were. She would trust that the shelter was where he said it was.

They began walking up the riverbed, one slow step at a time. Within just a few minutes Tanner wasn't even trying to keep his weight off her. When he began wanting to rest, she knew they were in even bigger trouble. If Tanner sat down, there was no way she was going to be able to get him on his feet again. Tanner finally collapsed completely against her just about the time they rounded a corner and she saw the bridge.

"Tanner, there's the bridge. We're almost there."

"Leave me," he whispered.

Bree just rolled her eyes and kept walking forward. "Don't go all martyr on me now. If I was going to leave your heavy, muscled ass it would've been half a mile ago."

He didn't respond. And he stopped walking. That wasn't a good sign.

"Can't. You go."

Bree got in front of him again, grabbing him by his soaked shirt, careful not to hurt any of his many injuries. She was going to use his greatest weakness against him and didn't even care if that made her a bitch.

"You want me warm and safe inside that shelter, Hot Lips? Then you keep going. Because if you stop here, I stop here. That's it. End of story. Dig deep for me, baby."

His expression didn't change, but he started walking again.

She couldn't even see the crude door until they were right up on it. It was a small shelter that had been built into the highest section of the river's ravine walls. Unless you knew it was there, you'd never guess that was what it was.

She was carrying almost all of Tanner's weight the last dozen yards up the trail. He was almost unconscious on his feet.

And that damn storm never let up.

Leaning Tanner up against the side of the shelter, she pushed the heavy door open the only way she could, by throwing all her weight against it.

Nothing came flying, slithering or growling out. Anything else she didn't care. Grabbing Tanner on his good side before he fell face-first, she eased him inside the door. Then helped him as best she could down to the ground.

He was out cold.

"You made it, Lips." Not that she'd ever doubted he would. Not when it came to keeping her safe too.

She kept the door open to try to look around the shelter in the dark. There wasn't much. But what there was, was beautiful.

In one corner were five blankets wrapped and sealed in plastic. In the other corner, at least a dozen cans of food and a couple of can openers. She wouldn't be able to start a fire to cook whatever was in the cans, but she would gladly eat it cold at this point.

But first she had to get Tanner warm.

When she stumbled to the blankets and was assaulted by dizziness, she knew she was on the last of her own reserves. Tanner hadn't been the only one to draw on every remaining bit of strength.

She pulled the blankets over near him and began stripping off his clothes. He wasn't shivering—that was a bad sign. She dragged off every piece of clothing, then did the same for herself. Fingers nearly numb, she ripped open the packages containing the blankets. She immediately began wrapping them around Tanner, starting with his feet and head. She wasn't sure if what she was doing was technically right but figured anything had to be better than his cold, wet clothes. When she'd wrapped three blankets around him, she lay down beside him and wrapped the final two around them both.

And then she rubbed. She rubbed his chest and shoulders with her hands. She rubbed his legs with her feet. She rubbed her body all over his.

If he was awake, he would've teased her unmercifully about her gyrating, but at least it was creating warmth between them.

She rubbed until she wasn't able to find the energy to move anymore, then tucked his hands between their stomachs, and his feet between her calves.

She slept in fits and starts over the next few hours. At one point she got up and opened herself a can of what ended up being black beans, eating it with no hesitation whatsoever right out of the can using her fingers. But when she tried to wake Tanner up to get him to eat, he didn't even budge, not even when she wrapped his bullet graze with some gauze she found.

Shouldn't he be waking up? What if he had a concussion? Internal bleeding? She still had him wrapped in the blankets. It wasn't unbearably cold now that they were dry and out of the elements, but still his skin was cool to her touch. How many times this past winter had she called him her personal electric blanket, always rolling in toward him seeking out his warmth? But it wasn't there now.

Darkness had fallen, and there was nothing she could do right now anyway. If he still hadn't woken up by first light, she'd have no choice but to leave him and try to get help herself. She lay back down, pulling his body close to hers, resting her hand over his heart, assured somewhat by its strong, steady beat.

So many variables came into play, so many things that could still go wrong. Of course, she and Tanner had had all sorts of variables—good and bad—laid out in front of them before, and they'd always dealt with them one by one because…

Bree sat straight up, then lay back down.

She had her vows.

Just like that, they'd come to her. Right here, lying naked on the ground after eating a cold can of beans, she'd finally figured out her vows.

They'd been right in front of her all along.

She wrapped Tanner tighter in her arms.

Now she just needed to have the man with her in five days to say them to.

Chapter Eighteen

Tanner lay on the cold hard floor, consciousness coming back slowly. The first thing he became aware of was Bree pressed up against him, but that wasn't unusual. She was almost always the first thing he became aware of when he woke.

The second thing was that he wasn't cold. There'd been a time trudging up that riverbank where he was sure he would never be warm again.

He seemed to have all his fingers and his toes, so that was a good sign. Honestly, he was just surprised he was alive. He'd been sure he wouldn't make it. If it hadn't been for the fact that he knew Bree wasn't going to leave him, he'd be dead right now out in that water.

She sighed and moved against him, quickly proving the rest of his body was working just fine also, as her naked skin brushed against his.

She'd killed a man. In the midst of attempting to survive there had been no time to process that. He knew what it was like to take a life and wasn't going to allow her to feel any guilt over it. If she hadn't shot when she had, Tanner would be dead. She'd saved his life multiple times yesterday.

He pulled her closer until she was half lying on top of him, her favorite way to sleep. She let out a shuddery little breath and his heart clenched. He knew that sound. It was the sound she made when she had been crying. It didn't happen very often—for the longest time Bree had a difficult time accessing her feelings at all—and the sound gutted him now.

When he trailed his hand down her back, she shifted against him. "Tanner?"

"You went to an awful lot of trouble just to get me naked here with you, freckles."

She bolted upright. "You're awake!" She rubbed her face with the back of both hands. "I didn't mean to fall asleep. I'm not a very good watchman."

"You've got that gun right by your lap. I daresay if anyone came to that door you would've woken up. Your body needed rest."

He wanted to ask her why she'd been half crying in her sleep, but she was already starting to inspect his body for injuries.

"Your shoulder is definitely dislocated. If I had my computer, I could look up how to put it back into joint, but now it's so swollen you really need a medical professional."

He definitely already knew that from the fire shooting down his arm and chest every time he moved.

"I'll try to make some sort of sling out of your jacket. I don't know if that will really help, but it should at least take some of the weight off your shoulder," she continued. "I also think you have a concussion, but there's nothing I can do about that."

"Nothing is life-threatening—that's the most important thing, okay?" He trailed the fingers of his good hand up and down her arm. "Given the fact that I was shot at, fell over a ravine and was nearly clubbed to death, not to mention hypothermia... I feel pretty damn lucky."

She nodded. "You have to be hungry. There are some cans of food. Nothing particularly appetizing, especially since we've got no way to heat it up. But at least filling. I have no idea who keeps this place stocked, but the food isn't expired."

"Old man Henrikson. He lives just outside town, but comes through once a year and makes sure the three or four shelters in this area have some basic provisions."

"Henrikson? Who would've figured the most ornery man in town was a good Samaritan."

"When his grandson was a teenager, he got caught out in a freak June snowstorm. Broke his leg, couldn't get back home. He would've died if it hadn't been for a shelter that happened to be stocked by a hunter who'd been in a couple weeks before. Henrikson has come out every year for the past twenty years to make sure these shelters in the area are stocked."

She kissed his forehead. "Hopefully that lovely story will make your cold franks and beans taste better."

He ate the can she opened for him, careful to keep

the Glock close to his side in case it was needed, while she laid their clothes out a little better to dry. Outside the rain continued to fall, although at least most of the thunder and lightning had stopped.

"How safe are we here?" she asked.

"This place is difficult enough to find in sunny weather. No one will stumble on it in this rain. It's possible they would know about it if they researched hiking and hunting up here, but otherwise I wouldn't count on anyone coming through that door."

Tanner remembered the maps he and Noah had seen Jared and his friends looking at the night they'd surveilled the town house. Could they have been looking at trails and shelters around here? It would've explained a lot: how they'd known where the rafts would be located, and the best place to puncture them. They could've studied the best places to try to ambush them.

He realized that Bree was sitting just out of reach, smoothing out the legs of his pants, then doing the same to hers. Her movements were jerky, almost frantic.

"Freckles, come here and sit by me."

"Why? Are you hurt? Why didn't old man Henrikson put some ibuprofen in the shelters, for goodness' sake?"

He smiled and held out his good hand. "Actually, I'm sure if you mention it to him, he will."

"Well, that's not exactly going to help you, is it?" Her voice was tight. Shaky.

"Bree." He patted the space beside him. "I'm okay. Come sit with me."

She did, although a little reluctantly. "We need to get back into town."

"We will. We've had rest, food. It will be much easier now. Let's just give the storm a few hours and see what happens."

If anything, that made her tenser.

He took her hand in his, twining their fingers together. "Why were you crying in your sleep, freckles? Not because of shooting that guy, right? His name is Paul Wyn. We have a file on him in the office and I recognized him when we were fighting. He's one of Jared Ellis's good friends."

Her eyes widened. "He was in Risk Peak the night of the fire. He'd been dressed as a paramedic and tried to get me to leave Sam and Eva with him while I got looked over in the ambulance."

Tanner let out a low curse. "Yeah, I think they knew about this trip and have been planning a kidnapping the whole time. But you shouldn't feel guilty about shooting him. You know you had to do that, right? He would've killed me."

Tanner would give anything if he could take that weight off her. Carry it himself. Taking a life, even in self-defense, or defense of a loved one, was still weighty.

But evidently, not too much to Bree. "Oh, no, I know I had to shoot him. He definitely would've killed you with that club. Honestly, if I had had a clear shot while you were fighting, I might have taken it."

Tanner let out a short bark of laughter. God, he loved this woman. She was so damn practical.

"Well, as a law enforcement officer, I'm much happier that if you had to shoot Wyn, you did it when he was about to kill me, rather than when we were fighting. That's much more defensible in my report." He rubbed her hand. "If that wasn't it, then why the tears? You were crying in your sleep."

"It's nothing." She looked away.

"Freckles, you're the least prone person to hysterics that I know. So if you're crying in your sleep, it's a big deal. Is it everything we've been through in the last couple of days? That's understandable."

"No, I—I... Forget it. Don't worry about it. Let's just worry about you getting back home in one piece. I'm fine."

Now he was really worried. He hadn't even thought to ask her if she'd been injured in some way. Was she hurt and trying to play it off?

He swallowed a groan of pain as he shifted his weight so he could get a better look at her.

"Tanner, what are you do—"

"What aren't you telling me? Are you hurt?"

He didn't see any marks on her naked body, but a lot of her was covered in blankets. "Bree?" He caught her chin in his hand, forcing those green eyes to look at him. "We're a team, right? That means you tell me when you need help too. It goes both ways."

His heart sat heavy in his chest as big tears rolled down her cheeks.

"Fine," she finally murmured. "I was crying because I was relieved, okay?"

That definitely wasn't what he'd been expecting. "Relieved that we made it to shelter? That we are warm and dry?" That made sense, but why not just admit that?

"No, relieved that I finally came up with my wedding vows!"

She closed her eyes and bowed her head as if she'd just admitted to committing the most atrocious of crimes.

"You were crying over our wedding vows?"

"You do know we're getting married in four days, right? And we have to say vows." Her whole body seemed to deflate. "I've just been in a state of panic, thinking of standing up there in front of everyone... I'm already such a social spaz, and you're so important in Risk Peak. I wanted my vows to be perfect so I don't embarrass you in any way. It's just been stressful."

He trailed his fingers down her cheek. "More stressful than running through the wilderness with people trying to kill you?" Because she hadn't cried then.

She tilted her head, obviously seriously considering the stress levels of both. "Actually, about the same."

He wanted to yank her to him but couldn't force his left hand to work at all. Instead, he threaded the fingers of his right hand into the hair at the nape of her neck. He'd known the wedding planning had been stressful for her but had no idea she'd been feeling such pressure about the ceremony itself.

He leaned his forehead against hers. "If you got up there and couldn't say a single thing except 'I do,' I wouldn't care. All I care about is that you're willing to give me forever."

"I do. I do want forever. But everyone you've known your whole life is going to be there. All your people. I just don't want to mess it up."

He'd been selfish. He'd wanted a big wedding— talked her into it and why?

Because he'd wanted to make his declaration of love for and commitment to her as public as possible. But he should've taken into consideration more what she really wanted. Bree could barely stand to be around a group of people at the best of times. And standing up in front of five hundred of them, many of them she barely knew… No wonder this had been so stressful for her.

He leaned forward and kissed her. "I never really thought about the wedding, the event itself, and how it would affect you emotionally. I've been joking all these months about taking you in front of the judge. Let's just do that. We don't need a big event. At the end of the day, our love, our marriage, is between you and me. Nobody else matters."

She smiled at him, the sight so beautiful and pure it nearly took his breath away. "Last week I might've taken you up on that. Hell, the night of the fire I almost got killed because I was in the office working on those stupid vows."

He smiled at her description. No one was ever going to accuse Bree of being overly sentimental. That was just fine with him.

"But they came to me while I was trying to sleep," she continued. "All this... And they just came to me. Honestly, that's why I was crying. I was just so relieved."

"Tell me them."

She reached up and kissed him softly. "I will. On Saturday. Four days."

He could wait. "Are you sure that's all that was upsetting you? You seemed flustered."

"I just want to get back so I can write all this down, so I don't forget them."

Tanner shook his head. "I've seen you memorize entire pages of coding after reading it just a couple of times. Your brain is like a computer."

"Exactly. I can remember coding, but words? Emotions? Not so easy."

He tucked her against his chest with his good arm, ignoring the pain as best he could in the other. "If you're worried you won't be able to remember the words, just write a program in your mind that includes them."

"What? I—" she paused. "Damn it, Dempsey, you're a genius."

She lay down next to him and he could almost hear her brain running like a machine. He had no idea what program she was writing, or what it would do, but knew whatever information she needed was now safely locked away in that brilliant mind of hers. When she slept this time, there were no tears.

Chapter Nineteen

Two shots firing into the air woke Tanner immediately. He and Bree had changed back into their clothes as soon as they were dry in case they had to run again. They'd slept side by side, but without her curled up next to him. The slightest touch on his left arm sent spikes of agony through his system. And he'd wanted to have his right arm free in case he needed to get to the Glock quickly.

Five minutes later shots rang out again.

"Freckles, wake up."

"I don't want any more beans," she muttered, not opening her eyes.

"We've got to get moving."

Now those green eyes popped open. "Did they find us?"

"Not the hunters." He forced himself to stand, bent over because of the low ceiling and, tucking the gun inside the waistband of his pants, took a look outside.

No more rain.

Two more shots.

"Was that a gun?" She joined him at the door.

"Yes, a signal from Noah."

"Are you sure?"

"Yes. The double shot, just like how we used the flare gun. He's signaling to let me know where he is."

"Won't that let the hunters know where he is too?"

Tanner nodded. "He wouldn't do it if he wasn't sure it was safe. I'm assuming he has backup. Normally I would use our gun to fire two shots in response, but I'd rather save those last two bullets in case we need them."

WHEN THEY FOUND Noah two hours later, he had more than enough backup. Sheriff Duggan, Whitaker and half the Grand County Police Department was with him. Not to mention two forest rangers and four citizens from Risk Peak who had exceptional experience in these woods, including old Mr. Henrikson.

And thankfully, a paramedic. Tanner's shoulder was the first line of business. There were things he still needed to do here before he could leave and go back into town.

Bree sat across from him, holding his good hand like they were about to arm wrestle, keeping his eyes pinned with hers as the paramedic rolled the swollen joint back into place.

Tanner's curse was low and ugly, but his eyes never left Bree's and she never flinched.

His shoulder immediately felt better, and he let go of her hand.

"I'm going to read up on how to do that," she said. "That's a good skill to have."

"And I hope one you'll never actually need to use."

Somebody offered him some ibuprofen and he took double the recommended dosage. His jacket would have to continue to second as a sling until he could see a regular doctor. But first there were things he needed to do here.

Noah looked almost as rough as Tanner felt when Tanner found him talking to Whitaker.

"Marilyn and the kids safe?"

"Yes. Ronnie Kitchens is keeping them in protective custody until we can prove who's behind this. I got her and the kids to Henrikson's house. Cass— I have to admit, I love our sister—had already sent somebody up there when Barb and Francis arrived and told her about the raft and the bridge being out."

"That was smart."

"At that point Cass still thought it was regular wilderness camping snafus but knew we'd head for Henrikson's house if we got in trouble. So she sent a phone with him, and once Marilyn was there, she sounded the alarm."

Tanner took a closer look at his brother. "You're looking a little bruised up. Run into a tree?"

Noah led Tanner off to the side where they could talk privately.

"I immediately came back out here to see if I could help you and Bree. Ran into a hunter who thought that his knife and my lack of one gave him an advantage. I'll be needing to take you to that body so you can do whatever cop paperwork is involved. I haven't mentioned it to anyone else because…"

Because Noah hadn't been sure how Tanner wanted to handle this. Because Noah still thought as a warrior; he'd never thought as a cop. And if Tanner just wanted these bodies to disappear, Noah would be willing to make that happen and never speak of it again.

"I'm going to have my own cop paperwork involved with the death of Paul Wyn, the guy Bree shot. Ends up he was in Risk Peak the night of the fire. So we'll report them both to Whitaker and process them officially."

"I didn't get a positive ID on my guy," Noah said. "But I'm sure it was another one of Jared's posse. You know he's behind all this."

Tanner ran his good hand over his face. "Yeah, but proving it won't be as easy."

After convincing Bree to let someone take her back to town so she could reassure Marilyn and the kids that everything was all right, Noah and Sheriff Duggan headed toward one body and Tanner and Whitaker headed for Paul Wyn, finding him washed up downstream not far from where Bree had shot him.

Since he'd been involved with the situation, Tanner stayed to the side as Whitaker inspected the body, giving Whitaker the short version of everything that had happened.

"I sort of wish fewer of my murder cases involved you, Dempsey."

"At least you're not trying to arrest me for this one."

Whitaker looked up from where he was crouched over the body and gave him a smirk. "Not yet."

The man had been sure Tanner was involved in a series of murders a few months ago. But Tanner couldn't really blame him for that since someone had been going out of his way to frame Tanner.

Night was falling once again by the time both bodies were ready to be escorted back into town. Given the circumstances, and the number of witnesses involved, there wouldn't be any charges filed against Bree or Noah.

And given that the second body was George Pearson, also someone tied to Jared Ellis, Sheriff Duggan had ordered around-the-clock protection for Marilyn. Although Tanner suspected Noah would be providing that also.

Ronnie already had a report for Tanner and Sheriff Duggan when they stepped into the office. Jared's ankle monitor had not shown any unusual activity. Denver PD had already been to question Jared. Evidently he, Oscar Stobbart and Marius Nixon, the friend who had paid Jared's bail, had all been together for the past forty-eight hours, working on a business plan.

Willing to vouch for one another's whereabouts 100 percent.

The next day Tanner and Sheriff Duggan called

in every favor they could and finally got a judge who was willing to have an emergency in-chambers session to hear the details that afternoon.

With one signature, Judge Osborne could require Jared to remain in jail until his trial, set for four months from now. Tanner was already sitting in the judge's chamber when Jared and Oscar Stobbart arrived.

And really wasn't surprised when he saw Oscar's hands had all sorts of cuts and abrasions on them, just like Tanner's.

Colorado wilderness can be a real bitch, can't it?

The judge entered and asked for Tanner to provide a summary of what had happened and what he was requesting. Tanner had already provided this to the judge in written form but forced himself to stay calm and focused as he reiterated the events.

What had happened in the wilderness. The two dead bodies lying in the morgue.

When Tanner was done, Judge Osborne asked Oscar for Jared's rebuttal.

Oscar's voice was solemn. "We are terribly sorry to hear about these awful events, Your Honor. But, respectfully, what does this have to do with my client?"

Ellis shot Tanner a smirk while the judge wasn't looking.

"Your Honor, both Paul Wyn and George Pearson are known associates—*recent* known associates— of Mr. Ellis's. And, as I mentioned in my report, I overheard two men talking who mentioned Jared by name, and that he wanted possession of the children."

Tanner wanted to mention the fact that one of the men talking had been Oscar but knew that that would derail the situation in a heartbeat, since Tanner hadn't actually seen him and couldn't prove it. He had to pick his battles.

"Again, respectfully, Your Honor," Oscar said, "Captain Dempsey has been through quite an ordeal. Could it be possible that he misheard, or misunderstood the conversation? Nor, as I'm sure you realized, has Captain Dempsey identified the speakers. We're not even sure that the two men he overheard mentioning the children were George Pearson and Paul Wyn, since Captain Dempsey never actually saw them. Beyond that, my client can speak only to his own whereabouts and intents."

"The two dead men are not just passing acquaintances of Mr. Ellis." Tanner took out a folder that contained pictures of Jared with the two men he had taken last week with Noah. "Here they were together just last week. They've known one another for years—they were some of Jared Ellis's closest friends. These were the men hunting Marilyn Ellis and her children."

Oscar let out a disappointed scoff. "Surveillance, Your Honor? It seems as if Officer Dempsey has a personal vendetta against my client. This is borderline harassment and it's part of a pattern. I'm not sure if you're aware of this, but last week Officer

Dempsey also brought in a civilian to study Mr. Ellis's ankle monitor."

"A civilian, but a renowned computer expert who has been utilized by law enforcement in the past," Tanner put in.

Oscar barely let him finish. "Officer Dempsey is determined to write Mr. Ellis's narrative the way he deems fit, not necessarily as the truth."

Tanner had been prepared for this.

"This is the only thing I'm interested in rewriting." Tanner slid another picture across the desk. "This is what Mrs. Ellis looked like during her last trip to the hospital. Jared Ellis gets his day in court for what he's been accused of. That's fine. But there was more than enough evidence to get a restraining order against him. The most important thing is keeping Marilyn Ellis and her children safe. And keeping Jared Ellis from doing something like this again."

"Allegedly, Judge." Oscar's voice was almost bored.

The judge turned to Tanner. "Did you see Jared in the woods? Do we have any reason to believe the ankle monitor is not working properly? You tell me that's the case and I'll sign the incarceration paperwork right now."

"Your Honor—" Oscar started until the judge held up his hand.

Tanner wanted to lie. More than any other time in his life he wanted to tell the judge there was reason to suspect Ellis could get out of the monitor. But he couldn't do it.

"Not specifically with Jared Ellis. But we can all admit that these monitors are not perfect."

"Actually, Your Honor, there has never been a reported case of this particular monitor being hacked or removed without intention. One hundred percent of the people who have attempted to remove this type of monitor had law enforcement at their location within minutes and were immediately apprehended."

The judge studied the reports on the technology Oscar handed him. Tanner knew the information was impressive. Hell, even Bree hadn't been able to figure out a way to easily hack it.

"Based on this data, I'm not going to put Mr. Ellis back in jail to await trial."

"Thank you, Your Honor," Oscar and Jared both answered in unison. Jared had obviously been coached not to say anything during this meeting.

"But if there is so much as a hint of any of Mr. Ellis's other *known acquaintances* creeping around Mrs. Ellis or the children, then you can expect to be spending the rest of your time in holding. Got that, Mr. Ellis?"

Oscar immediately broke into protest. "Your Honor, I highly object to holding my client accountable for others' actions."

Judge Osborne very calmly turned the picture of Marilyn's battered body back around on his desk, pushing it to the edge.

"Save your objections for the court, Counselor. I have a feeling you're going to need it."

The judge turned to Tanner. "Captain Dempsey, I will request that the Denver marshals' office send officers over daily to make sure Mr. Ellis isn't having any difficulties with his monitor."

"Your Honor!" Oscar protested again.

"Your client is getting to stay out of jail. I'd be happy with that and concentrate on how you plan to convince a jury he deserves to stay that way."

Oscar grumbled under his breath, but it was Jared who spoke.

"That's fine, Your Honor. I just want to get this whole misunderstanding behind me. I look forward to my chance in court to show what really happened."

The judge nodded, lips pursed. "Yes, I'm sure you do."

Oscar and Ellis left, and Tanner thanked the judge for his time. On his way back out of town, Tanner stopped by the Denver marshals' office himself. These were the ones who would be first on the scene if anything so much as beeped concerning Jared.

They had already heard what had happened over the past two days and took his concerns seriously. Jared's whereabouts were a top priority for them.

They even took the time to double-check the monitoring system, bringing Tanner to the room where Bree had worked last week. While Tanner watched, they got the coordinates of Jared's location, then sent an officer out to make sure that was correct.

It was.

By the time Tanner left, he wasn't thrilled that

Jared wasn't back behind bars, but at least he knew the people here cared what happened. It wouldn't be long before that bastard was behind bars for good.

Chapter Twenty

"It really is a beautiful dress, Bree. Tomorrow is going to be amazing."

Bree took a sip of her wine. She, Cassandra and Marilyn were sitting in her apartment, in three chairs across from the couch where her wedding dress was laid out carefully.

The rehearsal dinner had gone without a scratch. Yes, half the town had been there, but Bree had just been able to relax and enjoy it. After everything she and Tanner had been through, she didn't want her own wedding to stress her out. Like Cassandra had told her, if you did it right, you only got married once.

Looking over at Tanner tonight as he walked around the Sunrise Diner, where they'd decided to hold their rehearsal dinner, talking and joking with all their family and friends, Bree knew she was doing it right.

Tomorrow morning, she would become Mrs. Tanner Dempsey. Bree Dempsey.

When she'd first heard that unexpected knock on

her door in her nearly empty apartment in Kansas City, she'd never dreamed it would lead her here. To this place. To this moment.

But how thankful she was that it had.

Everything; the danger, the pain, the fear… It was all worth it because it had made them the Bree and Tanner they were now.

All those variables.

"What's that little smile?" Cassandra asked, taking another sip of wine.

It was after 10:00 p.m., the wedding was in the morning and her two best friends were here for a few more minutes. Tonight was her last night in this apartment. Bree doubted she would sleep very much, but that was okay.

"I'm ready," she said. "In every way that someone can be ready to marry someone else, I'm ready. It's time for Tanner and I to start our forever."

Cassandra let out a string of curses that would make a sailor blush, then burst into tears. "That's the most beautiful thing I've ever heard. And I love it even more that my brother feels the exact same way."

Marilyn smiled too. "It's going to be an amazing day." She turned back to the dress. "And that dress is just so…"

"Ornate?"

Marilyn chuckled. "It is ornate. It's beautiful, Bree. Of course, I got married in a denim skirt, so I'm probably a little bit partial to big, beautiful wedding dresses."

It still wasn't the dress Bree would've picked out

if she'd gone with her heart. But there was no doubt the dress was beautiful, and it would be beautiful tomorrow when she wore it down the aisle.

She was about to say so when a distinct beeping noise began shrieking from her computer. It took her a moment to realize exactly what it was.

Jared Ellis's ankle monitor had just gone off.

She scrambled over to her laptop and began typing in information. Not ten seconds later everybody's phones began beeping—they were all receiving the alarm she'd set up as an app on their phones.

Bree's phone rang and she lifted it to her ear as she continued typing.

"Are you looking up the details on Jared?"

She loved that Tanner knew her well enough to cut straight to the chase, even the night before their wedding, not wasting time with greetings.

"Yes. It looks like he's still at his apartment. So if it went off, it was because he was trying to remove it from his body."

"I'm calling the Denver marshals. Noah is on his way to your place already. I'll make the call and be right behind him."

Bree disconnected the call and looked over at Marilyn. Every bit of color in the other woman's face had leached out.

Cassandra rushed over to her, grabbing her hands.

Bree brought the laptop over so Marilyn could see it. "Look, the monitor is still on, and still in his apartment. I won't say there's no cause to be alarmed, but let's get all the information before we panic."

Marilyn nodded. "I need to get to the kids. They're asleep at New Journeys."

Cassandra nodded. "I'm going to call Barb right now and have her put the building on lockdown, okay? There's absolutely no way Jared could get in that building. Hell, the kids will be safer than we are."

Marilyn nodded and Cassandra got on the phone.

When the alarm on her laptop screeched again, Bree opened the program to see what new data had come in.

Jared's monitor was now offline altogether.

Before Bree could even give anyone the bad news, Noah walked through the door. He went straight over to Marilyn and pulled her against his chest.

"We've already got Ronnie standing guard over at New Journeys," he said. "The kids are safe."

"Jared's tracker just went offline," Bree told him.

"What does that mean, exactly?" Noah asked.

Bree looked at him and then at Marilyn. "Technically, it means we no longer know exactly where Jared is."

When Tanner walked in a few moments later, some of Bree's tension eased. He looked calm, not panicked the way she felt. He was on the phone with someone. Cassandra, always in wedding-planner mode, threw a blanket over Bree's wedding dress on the couch.

"I'll call Sowers myself if that's okay with you, Marshal, just to double check. I've got his number."

Tanner nodded as he listened to whatever the marshal was saying. "Will do. Thanks for calling us first."

Tanner ended the call. "Adam Sowers, one of the marshals I met personally two days ago, is already on scene. Everything is okay. Sowers was nearby when Jared's alarm went off and he got the call. He immediately went to Jared's town house, arriving within two or three minutes of the alarm. Jared was still there."

"The monitor is offline now," Bree said.

"Yes, Sowers confirmed this. Evidently Jared developed some sort of rash under the monitor. He was trying to loosen it to keep it from chafing and knocked it offline."

"You met this guy Sowers, and he's on the up-and-up?" Noah said.

Bree was already sitting down at her computer. She wanted to know everything there was to know about this Adam Sowers. There wasn't time to go through legal channels, so she just wasn't going to mention what she was doing to her husband-to-be.

"Yeah," Tanner said. "He's young. Enthusiastic about the job and about making a difference. I'm going to call him myself right now."

Bree didn't pay attention to Tanner's call. Tanner was much better at telling if someone was lying than she would be. She was good at digging up facts.

By the time Tanner was off the phone with Sowers a few minutes later, Bree was feeling much better about him too. Sowers seemed to be exactly what Tanner had said. He'd been out of the police academy and part of the marshals' office for two and a half years. He was married with a six-month-old daughter. No indication of any sort of questionable finances, infidelity or bad habits.

"Sowers is a good cop. I believe him," Tanner said from across the room.

"I concur," Bree said, closing her laptop.

Tanner narrowed his eyes at her. "Don't even tell me what you were doing. Do not make me arrest you the night before we're getting married."

"Moi?" She gave him her most innocent shrug, and he just rolled his eyes. She was pretty sure he wouldn't arrest her, but not 100 percent.

But at least it broke the tension in the room.

"It's really safe?" Marilyn asked.

"Jared will either go into holding until the ankle monitor can be fixed or someone will keep him under surveillance." Tanner gave Marilyn a kind smile. "We'll be notified if anything changes."

She still looked pretty worried, and after what she'd been through, Bree couldn't blame her.

Bree came over and rubbed Marilyn's shoulder. "This actually reassures me that the monitor is working the way it's intended. I don't doubt that Jared was probably trying to test it out and see if the cops came running to his door if he tried to remove it. Now he knows it works and they will."

Tanner slipped an arm around Bree's waist. "And we might be able to use this with Judge Osborne to get Jared moved back into jail until the trial. The judge isn't going to put up with this nonsense."

"I know I was supposed to hang over here with you tonight," Marilyn said. "But I just need to go check on the kids."

Bree pulled Marilyn in for a hug. "I'm fine. Go be with your kids. I totally understand. I'll just see you bright and early in the morning."

A midmorning wedding had seemed like such a romantic idea at the time Bree had let Cassandra and Cheryl talk her into it. And Bree had to admit that watching the sun make its way past her beloved Rockies was definitely her favorite time of day.

"Okay, I'll see you tomorrow. Get some sleep." Marilyn pointed at Tanner. "And you get out of here. You're not allowed to stay with her, because we all know what's going to happen if you do."

Tanner smiled. "Yes, ma'am."

Cassandra grabbed her jacket. "I'm going to head home to my family too. Wrap that dress back up as soon as we leave and hang it on your bedroom door. No point in inviting disaster. I cannot even think of red wine coming anywhere near it."

"Fine. I'll keep it safe, I promise." Marilyn hugged her again and Noah escorted her out the door, Cassandra right behind them.

Tanner walked to the door himself, then turned back.

"I don't suppose I could talk you into letting me see that dress," he said with a smile.

"Nope. Cassandra and Marilyn would both kill me. They think it's the most beautiful thing since sliced bread."

Tanner laughed but then the smile fell from his face. "But you don't?"

This was going to be the problem with being married to such a good cop. She wasn't going to be able to hide stuff from him. "You know me, not big on dressing up in girlie stuff."

"How about you wear that dress for me tomorrow morning at our wedding and I'll make it worth your while tomorrow night."

He held open his arms, ignoring his stiff shoulder, and she walked into them. "It's a deal." One she definitely didn't mind making. "And the dress is beautiful. It's gorgeous, even."

"You are what will make it gorgeous. It wouldn't matter what you wear."

He kissed her. Soft, sweet, light. The same sort of kiss he'd started with her all those months ago.

"That's our last kiss when we're not husband and wife," she whispered when they finally broke apart.

He leaned his forehead against hers. "I promise, the kisses just get better from here. But now I better get going or not only will that not be our last kiss—I might really decide I want one more last something else before we get married."

She gave him a scandalized grin. "What would Marilyn say?"

He smiled too and cupped her cheeks. "I'll see you tomorrow."

"I'll be the one in white."

"I can't wait. Lock the door behind me." He kissed her on the forehead and walked out the door.

Bree locked it, then turned and walked over to the couch and pulled the blanket off her dress. It really was beautiful. Not *her* maybe, but beautiful. It would make Tanner proud of how she looked when he saw her in it. And that was close enough to perfect for her.

She walked into the small bedroom to get the plastic garment bag.

A knock on the door had her turning away. Maybe it was Marilyn having decided to come back. Good. She could help Bree get the dress into the garment bag. Or maybe it was Tanner wanting more kisses— that was even better.

But when she opened the door it was neither. Jared Ellis stood on her doorstep.

After a moment of shock, she tried to slam the door in his face, but he was too quick. His backhand caught her across the cheek, and she stumbled backward. He quickly took the opportunity to enter her apartment, closing the door behind him.

"You're going to help me get my wife back."

Bree spun around, running for her phone. Tanner couldn't be but half a block away. One message and he'd be back here in under a minute.

But then Jared pulled out a gun.

"If you grab that phone, I'm going to have to shoot you. That's going to be inconvenient for me and painful for you."

She was tempted to go for the phone anyway. Given what she knew about Jared, being shot may be more of a mercy than some of the other things he was capable of.

He grabbed her and threw her onto the couch—onto her beautiful wedding dress—before she could make a decision.

"How did you fool the monitoring system?" she asked, keeping her eyes on the gun still trained at her.

Bree wasn't conceited, but she found it nearly impossible to think that this guy had found a way around the system that she had missed.

"It's all about weaknesses," Jared said. "Pressure points in the system. I'm very good at finding pressure points."

"The system didn't have any pressure points. I searched it myself."

He gave a shrug and cocky half grin. "The computer system wasn't the weakness. It only needed to be circumvented."

He pulled up the leg of his khaki pants to show the monitor was gone.

"So that alarm I got was correct. You had taken it off. You must have bribed Sowers. He lied about you still being in Denver."

Jared shrugged. "*Bribe* is not really the correct word. Like I said, I'm very good at finding pressure points. Sowers's is his wife and newborn daughter. Once I applied a little pressure to that point, he was willing to do whatever I wanted, including say he was still with me if anybody called."

His eyes were so cold. So dead. This man was a sociopath.

He pointed the gun a little closer at her. "I'm going to need you to call my Marilyn."

There was no way in hell.

"She won't answer. Thanks to your little stunt, when we got the alarm that there was something wrong with your ankle monitor, she went into hiding with the kids."

His eyes narrowed. "But surely she'll come if her dear friend needs her the night before the wedding. Maybe tell her you got cold feet, you need her to help you figure out what you should do."

"You don't think she's going to be a little suspicious of that? An hour ago I couldn't wait to get married, then all of a sudden I'm calling saying I'm about to skip town? Oh, and it just happens to be when there was indication that you were messing with your ankle monitor. Hmm, I wonder if she'll be suspicious about that at all. I wonder if maybe she'll go to the police. I wonder if maybe you've underestimated Marilyn for way too many years and she's never going to put herself in a position where you have control over her again."

Bree spit the words out and finally got some real emotion in his eyes. *Anger.*

"I'm not afraid of you," she lied with a steady voice.

But she was. He had a gun. And she might know some self-defense moves, but most of them weren't going to do much good against someone determined to shoot her.

Jared shook his head. "Marilyn used to be a lot

more like you when I first met her. Feisty. Wanted to fight back. But eventually I taught her to heel. She's very well trained now. Which is why I am, in fact, going to need you to call her and get her to come over."

Bree stood. No matter what he threatened, Bree wasn't going to allow Marilyn to put herself back in this man's clutches. "Even if she would come, which I don't think she's stupid enough to do, I won't do it. I won't call her. You'll have to shoot me."

For a second she thought he was actually going to do it, but a knock on the door stopped him.

"Bree, it's me. I couldn't leave you on the night before your wedding."

Bree's eyes met Jared's cold ones.

It was Marilyn.

Chapter Twenty-One

Tanner walked into Micky's, one of the two bars in Risk Peak. He'd had his first legal drink here when he turned twenty-one. It was only right that he'd have his last drink as a single man here also.

Noah would be buying him both.

"Marilyn and the kids okay?" he asked Noah as his brother joined him at the booth. "Can't blame Marilyn for being nervous after everything that's happened in the last week."

"Yep. Kids were sound asleep."

Tanner took a sip of his beer. "The way Marilyn looked when that alarm went off about Jared's monitor… I wouldn't have been surprised if she'd taken the kids and fled the country."

"I'm trying to give her whatever she needs to work through this at her own pace." Noah spun his beer around between his fingers. "But believe me, it's only out of respect for you that this situation hasn't already been completely handled."

"Let the justice system work its process." But Tanner grimaced even as he said it.

"What was that look for?"

"In some ways I would totally approve of you handling it yourself. I got the case files. I know Marilyn told us some about what Ellis did to her, but it's bad, Noah."

Noah stared down into his beer. "She's told me a little. Sick stuff. The physical abuse was what got him arrested, but the other stuff he did to her..." He trailed off. "And I don't even think she's told me all of it."

"Then I'm sure most of it isn't in the police report either. But hell, what is in the report is bad enough. Jared should be looking at eight to ten years."

Noah shook his head. "Not long enough, if you ask me."

"It's too bad we can't pin the stuff in the wilderness on him. Whitaker is still looking into that. He's gotten warrants to go through Paul Wyn and George Pearson's phone records and texts. If he can tie it to Jared, you know he will."

"Good. Accessory to attempted murder is going to hold a much longer sentence, I'm assuming."

"Yeah, and that would be much better because I really don't like how Oscar Stobbart seems so confident about the case. That Jared won't see jail time."

"That's his job, right? Hell, someone who's as good at this sleazy lawyer stuff as he is knows that the appearance of confidence can get them a long way."

"I thought that too. But it's almost like they have

a plan. They aren't worried at all. And that worries me. I know confidence is his business, but I have no idea how Oscar can look at this evidence and be so sure Jared's not going to jail."

"Maybe they plan on paying off jurors or something. I know most of Jared's accounts are frozen, but you know he has to have stuff stashed away somewhere."

"Yeah, I'm sure he'd be great at finding the weakest link in jurors." Tanner took a sip of beer, another thought coming to his head. "Or maybe they don't plan on going to trial at all."

"You mean making a run for it?" Noah's eyes lit up, and Tanner knew he relished the chance to go after Ellis if he ran.

Tanner shook his head. "He would have to go before the trial, but the ankle monitor is unhackable. Bree would've found it. You saw how quickly her program worked to let us know Jared had even messed with it tonight. There are no weak links in the computer system."

Damn it. Of course not. Jared knew that.

Jared wouldn't be looking in the computer system for weakness. He'd be looking for weakness in *people*.

At the end of the day, Jared Ellis was a *bully*. He wouldn't try to buy people off when attempting to get them to do what he wanted them to do. He would use what he knew worked best. *Force*.

Tanner pulled out his phone and hit Send on the last call he'd made.

Noah had already noticed Tanner's tension and was pushing his drink to the side. "Who are you calling?"

"A hunch. It may not lead anywhere."

Noah just nodded.

The call went straight to voice mail. Tanner tried it again, but the same thing happened. Sowers wasn't answering.

"Adam Sowers, the guy who was checking on Jared, isn't answering."

"You think that means a problem?"

"I just don't like it," Tanner said. He tried one more time for good measure, but still nothing.

His next call was to Marshal Brickman to see if Sowers had checked in.

"Dempsey. I don't have any new information for you. I assure you, as soon as I have info, you'll be the first to know."

"Marshal, has Sowers checked in? I just tried to reach him on his phone and there was no answer multiple times. I was wondering if you'd heard from him."

"I personally haven't. Hold while I get in touch with the appropriate person."

Tanner pushed his beer to the side as he waited for the marshal to come back. He'd definitely lost his taste for it.

"Nobody has heard from him. I'm sending someone over to Ellis's house right now."

But if Jared was doing what Tanner was afraid he

might be doing, sending more officers to the town house wasn't necessarily going to help.

"Instead of sending someone to Ellis's place, will you send someone over to check on Sowers's wife and baby?"

There was silence from Marshal Brickman for a long moment. "What exactly do you think is happening?"

"I'm just wondering if maybe Jared Ellis didn't find a weakness none of us were considering."

"Adam Sowers is a good man. A good cop."

"Everybody has their weakness. We all know that's true."

Marshal Brickman muttered a curse. "Fine. I'll keep you posted if we find anything of interest."

Noah was already paying for the beers by the time Tanner disconnected the call.

"This all may be nothing," he told his brother. "I could be grasping at things that aren't there."

"Until we know that for sure, I think we need to head back to New Journeys. No harm in checking on Marilyn and the kids and standing guard there until we have multiple eyewitness accounts that Ellis is, in fact, still in Denver."

"I don't want to get Marilyn nervous if there's no reason to."

Noah shook his head. "Believe me, I don't want to either."

They rode together in Tanner's SUV to New Journeys. Both of them were checking the darkness for anything unfamiliar, person or otherwise, as they walked to the door. Tanner rang the bell, keeping his face clearly in range of the security camera so whoever was checking it would know it was him. Within just a few seconds the door was opening.

"Hi, Tanner," Francis said. "Bree isn't here."

He smiled. "I know. Actually, we're looking for Marilyn and the kids."

"She's not here either."

Noah's head shot around. "What? I just brought her back over here myself not even an hour ago."

The woman shrank back a little at Noah's tone. Tanner provided his most reassuring smile. "How about the kids? Are they here?"

Had they misread Marilyn? Had she decided to make a run for it since it looked like Jared might have made progress in attempting to escape his monitor?

"Yes, they're both in bed asleep. Marilyn went back out to see Bree. Said something about how she wasn't a marmot and that a good bottle of wine was a terrible thing to waste."

"That's good." Tanner smiled again, and the woman relaxed just a little bit. "It's good for Bree to have someone hanging out with her the night before her wedding."

Francis nodded. "That's what Marilyn and I thought too. Is everything okay?"

Tanner nodded. Noah had already gone back to staring out at any possible shadows in the darkness. "Yes, everything's fine. Just do me a favor. Call it prewedding jitters or whatever, but just don't open the door to anyone you don't know personally, okay?"

Francis smiled. "Trust me, I never do. But I'll make sure."

"I'll see you at the wedding tomorrow."

The door closed and locked behind him as Tanner turned and walked back toward his SUV with Noah.

"Maybe I'm looking for trouble that's not there. Maybe—"

The phone rang in his hand. "That's probably Marshal Brickman now. Telling me that Sowers requests that I stop being such an overprotective jackass and let him do his job."

Tanner pressed the receive button. "Marshal. I'm sure I probably owe you an apol—"

Brickman cut him off. "Dempsey, you were right. Ellis had someone holding Sowers's wife and baby hostage. Ellis is gone."

Brickman kept talking, but Noah and Tanner were already sprinting for his car. Jared was out and no doubt wanted to get his hands on Marilyn. And Marilyn might have led him straight to Bree.

Chapter Twenty-Two

Bree opened her mouth to scream and warn Marilyn, but Jared was expecting that. She ducked as his fist flew at her face, missing most of the blow, but it still caught her and spun her around back onto the couch. A drop of blood dripped from her nose.

Right onto her wedding dress.

That bastard had just stained her wedding dress. Who cared if she didn't like it—it was still *her* damn wedding dress.

"You keep the hell quiet." Jared stormed over to the door and yanked it open. Before Marilyn could do so much as give a terrified little shriek, he yanked her inside and shut the door behind her.

Bree's heart broke at the abject terror that carved itself into Marilyn's features at the realization that she was once again in this madman's power.

"Well, I guess this solves the whole problem on how to get you over here," Jared sneered. "Hello, wife."

Marilyn darted for the door, but Jared just snagged an arm around her waist, then flung her against the wall like she was a rag doll. "So predictable. You're always so predictable and stupid, Marilyn. It's why you'll always belong to me. You should be happy I even want to keep you."

Marilyn seemed to almost collapse in on herself, wrapping her arms around the side of her head in a protective gesture. Bree didn't know if it was physical or emotional protection or maybe both.

Bree stood up. She wasn't going to sit and watch him batter her friend.

"You made me get a drop of blood on my wedding gown," she announced with a calm she didn't feel. "Do you know how hard it is to get blood out?"

She had no idea what she was saying. She was just trying to buy time. But buy time for what to happen? Tanner had no idea Jared was in Risk Peak, and Marilyn obviously wasn't going to be in any shape to provide assistance against her ex.

Jared tilted his head to the side and directed the gun straight at her. "I think a spot of blood on your precious gown is the least of your problems. You're not really needed anymore."

"Jared—" Marilyn pushed herself off the wall.

He turned and pointed a finger at her. "You shut up. It's your fault that we're in this situation to begin with. Deciding to air all our dirty laundry with the cops. Every couple has an argument here and there. You didn't need to bring the cops into it."

"Leave her alone and I'll go with you." Marilyn's voice was soft, but not shaky.

"Marilyn." There was no way Bree was letting her leave with him willingly. "No."

Marilyn just ignored her, keeping her eyes trained on Jared.

"You leave Bree alone and you don't try to have any contact with the kids. That's the deal." Marilyn took another step toward Jared. "You want me to go with you, that's what you have to do."

Jared's cold eyes narrowed as he stared at Marilyn. He obviously wasn't used to her putting up any sort of argument.

"What's to stop me from killing her right now and dragging you anywhere I want to go?"

"Because if you're going to start killing, I'm going to start screaming my head off. I may not be able to stop you from killing her, but I will damn well make sure you go down also."

Marilyn took another step. Now Bree studied her friend more closely. Marilyn wasn't acting like Marilyn at all, and the truth became clear to Bree.

Marilyn wasn't going to wait for someone to rescue her. *She was going to rescue herself.*

Jared gritted his teeth. "Look at you. You get away from me for a few months and all of a sudden you're full of sass. Don't worry, I have lots of ideas of how to modify that behavior."

Marilyn flinched but didn't back down.

Jared took a step toward Marilyn and quick as a flash swung his fist with the gun toward the tiny woman's face. God, he was so quick.

Marilyn was quicker.

Tanner had been teaching Bree some self-defense moves, but it was nothing compared to what Noah had obviously taught Marilyn. She ducked under the punch aimed for her jaw. Jared obviously never expected any sort of countermove and had put all his weight behind the hit. It would've broken Marilyn's jaw, without a doubt, if it had connected.

Marilyn brought her knee up to his groin at the same time she reached up with both hands and clawed at his eyes. Jared let out a roar before stumbling back, tripping over Bree's coffee table. She jumped out of the way as he fell back on top of her couch.

Bree couldn't care less about her wedding dress under the man. He'd just dropped his gun.

Marilyn reached down and grabbed it, pointing it directly at Jared.

"You bitch!" Jared was clutching at his bleeding face. "You stabbed me with those claws of yours."

"Congratulations, jerk," Bree said. "You just graduated from assault and battery charges to attempted murder. You're going away for a long, long time."

Bree glanced over at Marilyn. The woman was pale, but steady.

Jared's face turned purple with rage. He reached into his pocket and pulled out a switchblade, flicking it open with his wrist.

"I don't think you're really going to shoot me, Marilyn." He stood up. "I think if you had really wanted to get away from me, you could've done that. Couldn't you have? I mean, how hard would it have been to leave for good? You stayed in the same state I was in. That's how I knew you didn't really want to get away from me. That you remembered how I rescued you when you needed it."

Marilyn's hand with the gun began to shake.

"Don't listen to him," Bree said. "You made the best decisions you could in the situation you were in. It doesn't matter what happened then. It only matters what happens now."

Jared took a step toward Marilyn. Bree wanted to grab her phone and call Tanner but knew there was no way he could get here in time, and she might distract Marilyn.

"If you take one more step, I'll shoot you," Marilyn said. But her voice was shaky. So very shaky.

"Come on now, sweetheart." Jared took another step toward her. "We both know you used up all your bravery on that little self-defense move you pulled a minute ago. How about if our deal still stands? You leave with me now, and nobody gets hurt."

Marilyn widened her stance and shook her head, her arm with the gun becoming steadier. "How about if Bree calls the police and you are out of my life for good? You'll never have me again, Jared. That teenage girl you rescued from the trailer park? I'm not that same person. I know my value. And I'm way too valuable for someone like you."

With a yell, Jared launched himself across the table, arm raised with the knife.

Marilyn didn't hesitate. She fired a double shot to the chest.

Shock blanketed Jared's features before he stumbled back and collapsed onto the couch.

Not a half second later both her front and back doors burst open, Tanner coming through the front, Noah the rear.

Bree just stared at him, the echo from the gunfire so close it caught her off guard. Processing seemed impossible.

Almost from a daze she saw Tanner checking for a pulse from Jared on her couch.

"He's dead."

It was Noah who came up to Marilyn and helped take the gun from her shaking hand.

Marilyn was staring at Noah with huge eyes. "You told me to attack at the beginning. That when he first saw me was my best chance for escape, but I froze. I froze."

Noah pulled her against his chest. "You didn't get him at the start, but you got him at the end. And when it's all said and done, that's all that matters."

Bree was still staring at Jared's body. Oh, God. He was on her wedding gown. Bleeding all over her wedding gown. She couldn't even think about that now.

Tanner was on his phone and soon all sorts of people were filing into her apartment. Ronnie, a paramedic, other people she didn't know.

Bree just stood there, almost numb.

Finally, it was Tanner's face right in front of hers that zapped her back into reality. "Freckles? You okay? Two dead bodies in one week is a lot for anybody to handle."

"I'm not sad he's dead. After what he did to Marilyn? This is the only way we'd know for sure he'll never hurt her again. He found a way around the ankle monitor. Something I missed."

Tanner shook his head. "He had Oscar Stobbart and Marius Nixon holding Adam Sowers, his wife and his baby hostage. That's how he got out of the ankle monitor—not something you *missed*, something you never even considered, because you're not a psycho like Jared. So Oscar will be going to jail for a long time too."

"Good."

She felt his fingers trail down her cheek. "Maybe we should get you checked out. You're looking a little pale. And you haven't taken your eyes off Jared since I got here. He can't hurt anyone anymore."

"I know. It's just that…he just bled out all over my wedding gown."

Chapter Twenty-Three

"They're supposed to leave tomorrow late afternoon for their honeymoon. It would be nice for them to be married before that happened."

"Not to mention there's no way we're going to get the church again any Saturday soon. It was hard enough to get it this weekend when we booked it six months ago."

"Plus, Bree's cousin Melissa and those sweet babies will be here only for this weekend."

Bree sat in a booth at the Sunrise Diner listening to the women talk around her, not even sure who was saying what. It was after midnight, her wedding dress was currently part of a crime scene and even if it was released, there was no way she was getting married in that thing.

Marilyn was sitting across from her in the booth, sipping coffee. They'd both already given their statements to the police. The fact that Jared had been coming at her with a knife when she'd shot meant there'd be no criminal charges brought up against

Marilyn. The woman had a lot she needed to process, but so far, she was holding up like a champ.

Marilyn had been sitting across from Bree for the past thirty minutes as more and more of the women from Risk Peak heard about what had happened and filled the diner around them.

"What's your plan?" Marilyn finally asked softly as the talking continued. "You know we can make the wedding work later if you want to wait. Don't worry about that."

But Bree didn't want to wait. She was ready. Ready for her always to start. Ready to say the vows that had become so clear to her.

Damn it. *Ready to have sex with Tanner.*

But she didn't want to do it without Marilyn up there with her. If she wanted to wait, Bree could wait too.

"What about you? I want you standing beside me when I do this. You've kept me sane over the past few months with all the wedding planning. If you're not up to it, then we'll reschedule."

Marilyn shook her head. "I refuse to give that man even one more hour of my life. Please get married tomorrow, Bree Cheese. Give us even more reason to celebrate *life*."

Around them someone was talking about whether they needed to wake up the church secretary right now and see if there were any other possible weekends available.

"No." Bree stood. Enough. "The wedding is still

on for tomorrow. As long as Tanner can be there, I'll still be walking down the aisle in the morning."

"Tanner will be there," Cassandra called out. "I already asked—since I'm the bossy little sister and allowed to ask questions like that. He says there's nothing about this situation that will keep him from the church if that's what you want."

But there would be no time to get another dress.

"I'll just wear a sundress or something," she said.

That was okay. The important thing was that she would get to marry Tanner tomorrow. She tried not to cringe at the thought of him in his tuxedo and her walking down the aisle in a sundress. But she didn't own anything fancier, and there was no way to get to a wedding dress shop before the ceremony in the morning.

"Oh, no you won't." Cheryl came and put her arm around Bree. How many times had she done that over the last year since Bree arrived in town? This woman had become a surrogate mother to her. Someone Bree treasured. "Leah and I have already been talking about that."

"You have?" Bree hadn't even realized Tanner's mother was here.

"We have a plan. We're going to make you a dress using sections of all of our own wedding dresses."

"But…I don't understand. Using pieces of your own dresses? Won't that ruin them?"

Cheryl pulled Bree in for a hug. "You're the only bride I know who's concerned about *our* wedding dresses, not about what *hers* might look like when it's all done."

Bree shrugged with one shoulder. "I can't envision it, to be honest. And is this even possible? How will you do it?"

"It won't be as ornate and detailed as your dress. There's no way we could make something like that probably *ever*, let alone in one night."

"Oh, well, that's okay. Nobody could actually make a dress like that one. I would never expect it."

"And would never want it either," Cheryl said with a smile. "Dan told me that as soon as he saw it. He admitted it was beautiful but said it wasn't a *Bree* kind of beautiful. I just wrote him off, convinced he was a man who didn't know anything about wedding dresses."

Bree couldn't stand that she might be hurting Cheryl's feelings after all the woman had done for her. "It is—*was*—a beautiful dress. Truly. I never would've picked out anything so beautiful without your help."

Cheryl smiled. "Oh, I know it was beautiful, but as painful as it is for me to say this, Dan was right. It's beautiful, but not a *Bree* kind of beautiful."

"I don't even know what Bree kind of beautiful is."

Cheryl reached in and kissed her on her cheek. "And that's exactly why it's such a unique beauty. Because you don't see it in yourself. Now, if you'll excuse me, I've got a wedding dress creation to supervise. We'll have you ready to walk down that aisle in the morning."

Bree squeezed her hand. "Okay. Thank you."

The older woman spun around and started announcing the plan. Everyone cheered, and within minutes they were running out into the darkness to grab their wedding dresses out of closets and moth-balls and cedar trunks.

Others were running off to grab sewing machines.

Someone grabbed Bree and pulled her into the middle of the floor and began measuring her around her pajamas.

Dan, the lone male voice in the whole place, yelled, "I'll start the breakfast food. Y'all are going to need it."

"And coffee!" Cheryl yelled.

"Of course coffee!" Dan returned with a grin. He winked at Bree as she held up her arms so someone could measure her bust. "It's not my first day."

Bree just watched it all with a smile. What else could she do?

The women came back, carrying their wedding dresses, laughing and joking and telling stories from their own wedding days. A few were telling interesting stories about the day they got divorced too.

None of them uttered a word of complaint as pieces of their dresses—usually parts of the train or underskirt that wouldn't ever be noticed, but sometimes more—were measured for the pattern they developed and cut.

It was the bodice of Gayle Little's dress that ended

up fitting Bree perfectly. The woman had lost her husband of sixty years just a few months ago. Bree couldn't even believe somebody Mrs. Little's age would be here helping in the middle of the night. But she was, and she was more than happy to provide this part of her dress, even though it meant taking the dress apart.

"I never had daughters. And it just wasn't the right style for the women my boys married," Mrs. Little said. "My Stanley would've been thrilled at the thought of you wearing it to marry Tanner. He always loved that boy."

Bree held the older woman's hand as Cheryl and the other seamstresses gently removed the bodice of Mrs. Little's gown from the skirt portion.

"You're going to make a beautiful bride, dear," she said.

The commotion continued around her and all Bree could do was watch and smile. Eventually she started serving food and coffee to the women who were working so hard for her.

It was nearing dawn when she found Cassandra on one side of her and Marilyn on the other.

"You okay?" Cassandra asked.

"I'm getting married in a few hours and it's going to be perfect." Bree had no doubt about it.

Cassandra nodded and put an arm around her.

"You were wrong when you said the church would tip over with Tanner's family," Cass whispered, looking around at the beautiful chaos surrounding them.

"I know. Because they're my family too."

Bree sat down in the booth where she'd first sat that day with the twins.

She'd been exhausted, at her lowest, empty.

And oh, so alone.

They'd helped her that day too, the people of this town. Her family.

She laid her head down on the booth table, just like she'd done that day. Her eyes closed as the sounds of laughter, talking and fellowship surrounded her.

Her family was here.

She woke to a gentle hand on her shoulder.

"Bree," Marilyn whispered. "The dress is done. It's time to get ready."

Bree looked out the window. The sun was already shining brightly.

"What time is it? How long did I sleep?"

How unfair was it of her to fall asleep while everyone else was working hard.

"I don't know. I conked out too."

Bree looked around. It was much quieter now, much less frantic. Three different sewing machines were still set up in the middle of the diner, but most of the women were now sitting around, drinking coffee and chatting.

Bree looked over at Cheryl. "I'm so sorry I fell asleep. I should have stayed awake and helped."

"Do you know how to sew?" Cheryl asked.

"No, but—"

"Then there wasn't any point in you being awake."

"Plus, we all know my brother is not going to let

you get any sleep tonight!" Cassandra yelled from across the room. Even Mrs. Little chuckled.

"Come try on your dress," Cheryl said softly. "It's hanging in my office."

Cheryl kept her office purposely dim as she and Cassandra helped Bree put on the gown, the tiny buttons traveling all the way up her spine taking the longest time to fasten. With every second Bree got more and more nervous.

Finally, they were finished, and Cheryl ran a smoothing hand over Bree's shoulders.

"Okay, let's go see if this was more like what you'd envisioned when you'd never envisioned what your wedding dress would look like."

Bree took a deep breath and followed Cheryl and Cassandra out of the room. It didn't matter. No matter what the dress looked like, Bree was going to smile and act like it was the most beautiful thing she'd ever seen.

The women had the full-length mirror set up in the middle of the dining area. Sniffles and murmurs broke out as soon as Bree stepped foot inside. She looked at Marilyn, knowing how much the woman had loved the other gown, trying to see if there was any hint of disappointment at seeing this one.

Marilyn was crying. That probably wasn't a good sign.

I love it. It's absolutely perfect.

She rehearsed the words in her head. No matter what, she would smile and tell them she loved it.

She looked at her reflection in the mirror and promptly burst into tears.

She was immediately surrounded by a gaggle of women.

"No crying on your wedding day."

"We know it's not as gorgeous as that other gown, but Tanner will be thrilled to see you in this."

"I think you look lovely."

Everyone was talking so fast and all over one another that Bree couldn't even pick out who was saying what.

"Ladies, give Bree a little space," Cheryl finally said. It was her diner, after all.

They quieted and stepped back so Bree could once again see herself in the mirror. She trailed her fingers from her shoulders down over her chest to her waist and hips.

Her dress was a rainbow of white. No one piece matched exactly with the next.

Her eyes met Cheryl's in the mirror, then Cassandra's, then Mrs. Little's.

"It's absolutely perfect. It's what I never even knew I wanted."

"Now there's a beautiful bride, right there." Mrs. Little stood beside Bree, looking at her in the mirror, wrapping an arm around her waist.

"There's a lot of love sewn into the dress you're wearing," the older woman continued. "Love the brides had for their grooms when they were first worn, and love for you, and what an important part of our community you've become. Now let's finish getting you ready, because I'm pretty sure there's a deputy captain who will arrest us all if you're not on time coming down that aisle."

Chapter Twenty-Four

By the time Tanner got to the church he was feeling a little like a zombie. Murder was a messy business in every possible way. Not just the physical part of it, although that was bad enough in this case. Making sure all the evidence was gathered properly, then working with the coroner's office to have the body removed.

Even in a cut-and-dried case such as this one, it was still labor intensive. Particularly since it was a murder that also involved a hostage situation in a separate county. So lots of hours of extra communicating and paperwork.

Whitaker showed up right before dawn to take over everything. Tanner let out a sigh of relief. He really hadn't wanted to miss his own wedding and honeymoon.

"Thank you, Richard," Tanner said as he shook the man's hand. He hadn't been required to come, since this wasn't the normal section of the county he worked in. He'd done so without anyone asking him to.

"I figured it was better for me to miss the wedding than you. But seriously, the next dead body? Please do not let it have anything to do with you or your bride."

"Deal."

By that point, there hadn't been any point in trying to get any sleep. Tanner tried to call Bree, to make sure she was okay.

He had no idea what he was supposed to say to a bride a few hours before her wedding when there was a dead body on top of her wedding dress. Even when he knew that bride probably better than anyone else in the world.

He just wanted to assure her that he was willing to do whatever she wanted to do. If she wanted to reschedule the whole thing, he would do that. If she wanted to get married in their jeans and T-shirts, he would do that. If she wanted not to have a big wedding at all, he would drag her in front of the judge in the next five minutes.

He just wanted her to know that he loved her.

But he didn't get to talk to Bree. Cassandra had answered the phone and explained to him what the women of the town were doing. She told him to hang out with Noah and to be at the church on time.

His breakfast with Noah had been pretty somber. A man was dead. And neither of them felt bad about it.

"Do you think Marilyn is going to be okay?" he asked in between bites of the breakfast food they had to get at the next town over because the Sunrise was currently a wedding dress factory.

"She'll have her ups and downs. Even knowing this was the only way she and the kids would truly be safe, it will still weigh on her. Make her wonder if there might've been a different way."

"Not in the eyes of the law. Ellis had every intent of hurting her and Bree, or worse."

Noah nodded. "That doesn't mean someone as tenderhearted as Marilyn won't still struggle with it. I would've taken that burden from her if I could."

Tanner wondered how long it would be before his brother realized he was in love with this woman. "I know you would, bro, but believe it or not, not all burdens are meant for you to carry."

"That woman has carried enough. She damn well doesn't need to carry any more."

Neither did Noah, not that he was going to be able to hear that. "Take a word of advice from your wise younger brother."

Noah snickered. "And what's that?"

"You two find a way of *sharing* the burden. I know that was one of the most fundamental lessons your time in the Special Forces taught you. A shared burden is easier to carry."

Noah nodded, then sat back and stared at him. "Dude, you're getting married in a couple hours. You nervous?"

"No." Tanner didn't hesitate. Didn't have any doubt. There was nowhere on earth he'd rather be than at that church watching Bree walked down the aisle.

And that was where he was two hours later when the wedding march played and Bree walked toward him slowly, escorted by Dan and Cheryl on either side of her.

Tanner knew he should look at her gown. Knew the women of the town had worked all night for Bree to have something to wear. But all he could see was her. It wouldn't have mattered what she'd been wearing— hell, it could've been a ten-thousand-dollar gown or a trash bag and he wouldn't have noticed.

She was stunning. She was perfect.

She was *his*.

And with every step she took toward him he was more in awe of that fact. When Dan flipped her veil over her head and she turned to him, trust and love shining out of those green eyes, Tanner felt it in every fiber of his being.

The minister said words, and Tanner repeated what he was supposed to and completed the tasks he was asked.

His eyes never drifted from Bree's face.

Only when it came time for the vows did he get snapped back into the ceremony. Bree had been nervous about this. With everything that had happened, they hadn't had much more time to talk about it.

He wanted to reassure her now that it didn't matter. That no matter what she said, he understood. That if she couldn't say anything at all, he would still know.

As Noah handed them both the rings, Tanner grabbed Bree's hands.

"We don't have to say anything if you don't want to," he whispered. He should've made this offer months ago and saved her so much stress. "We can just slip the rings on. You and I will both know what we're saying to each other without words."

Bree's smile was dazzling. "Don't worry. I've got this, Hot Lips," she whispered back.

The reverend indicated it was time for Tanner to say his vows.

It was easy for him. "You're every part of me I never knew was missing. Your intellect is astounding, but it's dwarfed by your beauty, your courage and your passion. I vow to cherish, honor and protect you all the days of the rest of our lives.

"You are my other half, my perfect fit, my forever partner. You are my greatest risk, my greatest reward, and I will thank God every day that you wandered into this town and not another."

A tear leaked out of Bree's eyes, but she was still beaming.

The reverend indicated it was her turn for the vows. She slid the ring onto his finger, but hesitated.

Tanner rubbed his thumb across the back of her small hand that was holding his. He would stay here as long as she needed him to. Or would help her out if she wanted. But mostly he would trust.

She said she had this, so he knew she did.

When the words came, there was no quaver, no problem being heard, no sign of nervousness. He would never have thought she could sound so confident in front of so many people.

He should've known better.

Her green eyes met his. "We both have known much loss in our lives, but we both found so much more. You are who I choose. You are who I choose to stand beside me when I need a partner, in front of me when I don't need a shield but you insist on being it anyway—" there were more than a few chuckles at that "—who I choose to stand behind me when I need support.

"I will fight back-to-back with you when our enemies surround us. I will fight shoulder to shoulder with you when injustice surrounds us. And I will fight face-to-face with you when you're being a jackass."

More laughs, and even he had to chuckle this time. Only his Bree could incorporate a mild swear word into her wedding vows so perfectly.

"You saved me in every possible way a person can be saved. You are my hero. And I know whatever risks the future brings, we will be fine."

She squeezed his hands, and her words slowed, took on depth. These were the words she'd found in the wilderness, he knew. "I don't care what all the different variables are, as long as the constant is us."

He kissed her. He was supposed to wait for the minister to say something, but he didn't care. She was his and he was hers.

The minister said something behind them and the

entire church broke into applause. The organ started playing the song they were supposed to exit to.

But it was only when Cassandra snickered and said, "Get a room," did Tanner finally let go of Bree's lips and open his eyes, finding her grinning just as hugely as he was.

He grabbed her hand and turned, walking her down the aisle to their forever.

* * * * *

Don't miss the previous books in USA TODAY *bestselling author Janie Crouch's miniseries, The Risk Series: A Bree and Tanner Thriller:*

Calculated Risk
Security Risk
Constant Risk

Available now from Harlequin Intrigue!

COMING NEXT MONTH FROM

⊞ HARLEQUIN®

INTRIGUE

Available October 22, 2019

#1887 ENEMY INFILTRATION
Red, White and Built: Delta Force Deliverance • by Carol Ericson
Horse trainer Lana Moreno refuses to believe her brother died during an attack on the embassy outpost he was guarding. Her last hope to uncover the truth is Delta Force soldier Logan Hess, who has his own suspicions about the attack. Can they survive long enough to discover what happened?

#1888 RANSOM AT CHRISTMAS
Rushing Creek Crime Spree • by Barb Han
Kelly Morgan has been drugged, and the only thing she can remember is that she's in danger. When rancher Will Kent finds her on his ranch, he immediately takes her to safety, putting himself in the sights of a murderer in the process.

#1889 SNOWBLIND JUSTICE
Eagle Mountain Murder Mystery: Winter Storm Wedding
by Cindi Myers
Brodie Langtry, an investigator with the Colorado Bureau of Investigation, is in town to help with the hunt for the Ice Cold Killer. He's shocked when he discovers that Emily Walker, whom he hasn't seen in years, is the murderer's next target.

#1890 WARNING SHOT
Protectors at Heart • by Jenna Kernan
Sheriff Axel Trace is not sure Homeland Security agent Rylee Hockings's presence will help him keep the peace in his county. But when evidence indicates that a local terrorist group plans to transport a virus over the US-Canadian border, the two must set aside their differences to save their country.

#1891 RULES IN DECEIT
Blackhawk Security • by Nichole Severn
Network analyst Elizabeth Dawson thought she'd moved on from the betrayal that destroyed her career—that is, until Braxton Levitt shows up one day claiming there's a target on her back only he can protect her against.

#1892 WITNESS IN THE WOODS
by Michele Hauf
Conservation officer Joe Cash protects all kinds of endangered creatures, but the stakes have never been higher. Now small-animal vet Skylar Davis is seeking Joe's protection after being targeted by the very poachers he's investigating.

———————————

YOU CAN FIND MORE INFORMATION ON UPCOMING HARLEQUIN® TITLES, FREE EXCERPTS AND MORE AT WWW.HARLEQUIN.COM.

HICNM1019

"Let's try this again." Logan wiped his dusty palm against his shirt and held out his hand. "I'm Captain Logan Hess with US Delta Force."

Her mouth formed an O but at least she took his hand this time in a firm grip, her skin rough against his. "I'm Lana Moreno, but you probably already know that, don't you?"

"I sure do." He jerked his thumb over his shoulder. "I saw your little impromptu news conference about an hour ago."

"But you knew who I was before that. You didn't track me down to compare cowboy boots." She jabbed him in the chest with her finger. "Did you know Gilbert?"

"Unfortunately, no." Lana didn't need to know just how unfortunate that really was. "Let's get out of the dirt and grab some lunch."

She tilted her head and a swathe of dark hair fell over her shoulder, covering one eye. The other eye scorched his face. "Why should I have lunch with you? What do you want from me? When I heard you were Delta Force, I thought you might have known Gilbert, might've known what happened at that outpost."

"I didn't, but I know of Gilbert and the rest of them, even the assistant ambassador who was at the outpost. I can guarantee I know a lot more about the entire situation than you do from reading that redacted report they grudgingly shared with you."

"You are up-to-date. What are we waiting for?" Her feet scrambled beneath her as she slid up the wall. "If you have any information about the attack in Nigeria, I want to hear it."

"I thought you might." He rose from the ground, towering over her petite frame. He pulled a handkerchief from the inside pocket of his leather jacket and waved it at her. "Take this."

"Thank you." She blew her nose and mopped her face, running a corner of the cloth beneath each eye to clean up her makeup. "I suppose you don't want it back."

"You can wash it for me and return it the next time we meet."

That statement earned him a hard glance from those dark eyes, still sparkling with unshed tears, but he had every intention of seeing Lana Moreno again and again—however many times it took to pick her brain about why she believed there was more to the story than a bunch of Nigerian criminals deciding to attack an embassy outpost. It was a ridiculous cover story if he ever heard one.

About as ridiculous as the story of Major Rex Denver working with terrorists.

Her quest had to be motivated by more than grief over a brother. People didn't stage stunts like she just did in front of a congressman's office based on nothing.

Don't miss
Enemy Infiltration *by Carol Ericson,*
available November 2019 wherever
Harlequin® Intrigue books and ebooks are sold.

www.Harlequin.com

Need an adrenaline rush from nail-biting tales (and irresistible males)?

Check out **Harlequin Intrigue®**, **Harlequin® Romantic Suspense** and **Love Inspired® Suspense** books!

New books available every month!

CONNECT WITH US AT:

Facebook.com/groups/HarlequinConnection

 Facebook.com/HarlequinBooks

Twitter.com/HarlequinBooks

 Instagram.com/HarlequinBooks

Pinterest.com/HarlequinBooks

ReaderService.com

 **HARLEQUIN®**

ROMANCE WHEN YOU NEED IT

SGENRE2018R

Love Harlequin romance?

DISCOVER.

Be the first to find out about promotions,
news and exclusive content!

 Facebook.com/HarlequinBooks

Twitter.com/HarlequinBooks

 Instagram.com/HarlequinBooks

Pinterest.com/HarlequinBooks

ReaderService.com

EXPLORE.

Sign up for the Harlequin e-newsletter and
download a free book from any series at
TryHarlequin.com.

CONNECT.

Join our Harlequin community to share
your thoughts and connect with other
romance readers!
Facebook.com/groups/HarlequinConnection

**ROMANCE WHEN
YOU NEED IT**

HSOCIAL2018